THE PAPARAZZO
AND THE POP STAR

AXIOM

The Paparazzo and the Pop Star

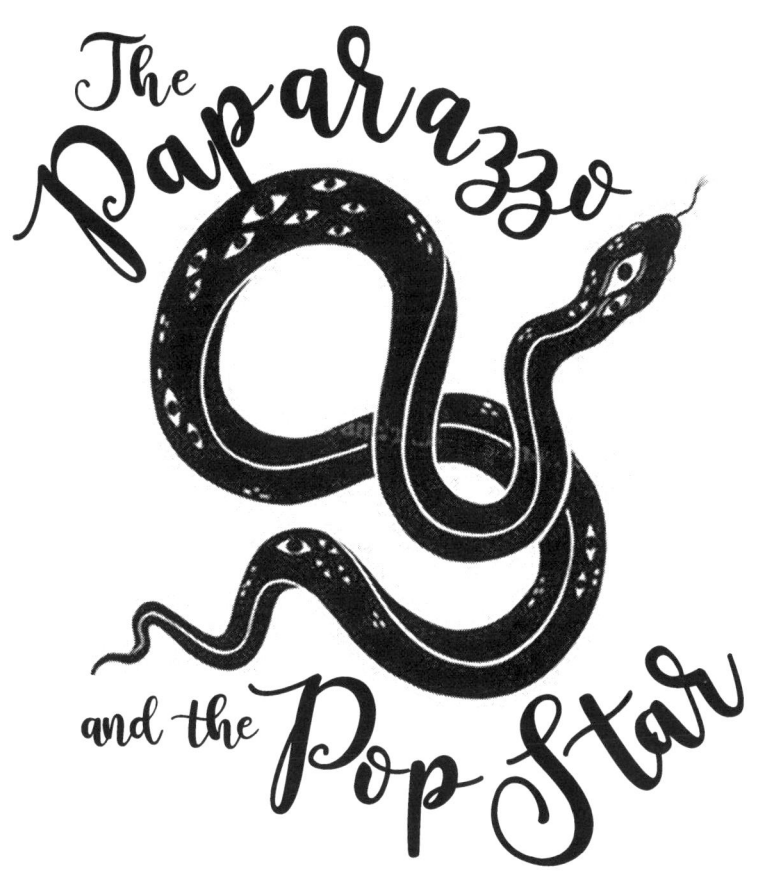

***A slightly raunchy yarn
of deceit and deception***

by Andrew Smith

For
Ros Martin (née Bates)
with love

When the person who'd followed Frank McCann up the stairs of the bus sat next to him, rather than in the completely empty seat across the aisle, Frank managed not to glare — he didn't even glance. Instead, Frank gazed out of the window at the dishevelled South London street and tried to remember exactly what had been said at the anger-management sessions that were a condition of his suspended sentence. Tamping down his irritation was all well and good, but if he made a habit of it, Frank swore he'd keel over with a heart attack, or be left a drooling wreck from a stroke.

"Frank ... bloody 'ell. Fancy banging into you then."

The realization that the man sitting next to him was his estranged daughter's husband did nothing to lower Frank's blood pressure. He detested Donovan Carter. But, knowing the report his son-in-law was sure to give to his daughter, Whitney, Frank managed not to scowl.

He glanced at Donovan's suit, noting that it was as tight and shiny as any worn by flash City boys he'd seen around London. Frank knew, from the days when he could afford made-to-measure, that a year's rent on his shabby bedsit — or 'studio apartment,' as the landlord insisted on calling it — wouldn't be enough to cover the cost of Donovan's outfit. He looked down to check the length of the trouser legs, and sure enough, not only were Donovan's sleek socks apparent, but above them Frank caught an unwelcome glimpse of his son-in-law's ginger-fuzzed leg, skin so white it was almost blue.

Even though he wished otherwise, Frank couldn't help but be aware that short-legged trousers were the current trend. He wondered if fashion designers were taking the piss, making trousers that looked like their owners had experienced an overnight growth spurt. For the money that the suit must have cost, Frank would have thought they'd have thrown in enough fabric for legs that reached Donovan's shoes, gleaming expensively from the shadows of the bus seat in front of them.

With Donovan's report of their encounter to Whitney in mind, Frank sat up straighter. He was super-aware that his old leather coat was the worse for wear, but he knew it fitted him well, and he was satisfied that the days when he could afford a gym membership were evident in his sturdy shoulders, deep chest, and muscular arms. He told himself he still had a vigorous head of dirty-blonde hair although he had to admit it had become more silver than gold of late. There wasn't much he could do about the porous quality of his skin. But Frank didn't think he looked quite so wasted since he'd eased up on the booze. Before Frank could steel himself to say something that wasn't unpleasant, Donovan rabbited on.

"I don't often make it down this way, Frank, but I 'ad to meet a new performer I just signed. Can you imagine, a musician wanting a meet at eight o'clock in the bleeding morning? But he's an ace remix man, best I ever 'eard. It's a different world now, Frank. Laptops and software is what it's all about these days."

Frank thought his expression — it had to be murderous — must have unnerved Donovan. But then Frank remembered his son-in-law always talked nineteen-to-the-dozen. It was one of the many traits that Frank found so irritating. He'd tried, God knows he'd tried. Frank knew perfectly well his first impressions, particularly those based on physical appearance, weren't always reliable. Unlike the accepted view that people wearing beer goggles must see everybody as if through rose-tinted lenses, Frank's alcohol-driven vision had only exaggerated people's flaws. So, when Whitney — his own beautiful baby-girl — brought home a freckle-faced, red-headed lad, shorter than her by at least six inches, and who burbled away like a hyperactive

Christmas elf with a battery that never runs down, Frank had taken an instant dislike.

"Give him a chance," Frank's wife, Christine, had said. "Anybody'd be nervous — the look on your face."

Frank turned his head away from Donovan to stare out of the bus window, hoping he'd take the hint and pipe down. He read the words on a jaunty sign boasting 'New Luxury Loft-style Apartments, from £990,000. Available Spring, 2012' that was posted in front of a Victorian brick building, newly scrubbed, the mortar of its red-brick facade neatly pointed. The thought that the price would have been well within his reach just a couple of years earlier depressed the hell out of Frank. Lately it had been all he could do to scrape together enough for his bus fare.

A mobile phone rang, an electronic version of what sounded to Frank like the soundtrack from a Bollywood movie. The feverish melody abruptly ended, and a second later the young woman sitting in the seat directly in front, her head and neck swathed by a vivid fuchsia headscarf, barked "Wot?" The prospect of having to overhear one side of an inane conversation didn't help Frank's struggle to repress the fantasy of giving Donovan's oversized hooter a swift head butt. The identical urge as last time he'd laid eyes on his son-in-law — or on his daughter, Whitney, come to that — two years earlier, after Frank's court case. Some frigging character witness Donovan turned out to be. His daughter's husband had done him more harm than good. The bitter memory came flooding back of how much it had hurt Whitney when, before his trial and pissed as a newt, Frank hadn't been able to hide his scepticism that Donovan could possibly be an executive of anything.

"He's vice-president of a flaming multi-million-pound record company. Of course he'll make a reliable character witness," she'd insisted.

Then, when she turned out to be so spectacularly wrong,

Frank's alcohol-fuelled character assassination of Donovan — justified or not — was the final nail in the coffin of his relationship with Whitney. The rift was a mile wide with little chance of repair.

Frank's shoulders relaxed slightly when the young woman in front ended her phone call as abruptly as she'd started it.

"I ain't goin' all the way to Slough just to get dissed by Jamal, innit," Frank heard her say before she stabbed her phone to end the call.

But Donovan seemed to take her silence as an opportunity to chatter on.

"I don't often take the bus, me. It's just that the Merc's buggered. Bastard car's only a year old too," he said.

Christ, but he was a tenacious bastard. If Frank was forced into having a conversation, he'd do it his way.

"How's my daughter?" he demanded.

"Who? Whitney?"

"You're not married to any other daughter of mine, are you, you stupid twat?"

"But you've only got the one daughter, Frank ... 'aven't you?"

Was Donovan trying it on, or was he really that clueless?

"Just tell me the last time you saw Whitney, my only daughter."

"Early this morning, lying in bed, kipping like a contented dosser, and snoring louder than a jumbo jet."

Frank thought he heard a snigger from the young woman sitting in front of them.

"Don't worry, I've never forgot, Frank, what you said to me the day we was married. About 'keeping your daughter in the manner to which she's accustomed.' It's just a crying shame you couldn't continue to provide for her yourself, isn't it, Frank?"

Frank grimaced. He felt his fingernails dig into his palm as he made a fist.

The bus shuddered to a halt on Battersea Park Road. A bevy of chirruping schoolgirls clattered down the stairs.

"But she don't want for nothing, Frank, believe me. Only the best for my Whitney."

Frank's other fist tightened. His Whitney, for Christ's sake.

"It's just lucky I've been able to keep ahead of the game, you know what I mean? Although, I don't mind telling you, Frank, times is tough, very tough indeed."

Donovan pinched his nostrils between thumb and forefinger. A nervous tic, Frank remembered.

"This is a ... forty-four bus to ... Victoria," said the posh lady on the loudspeaker as the bus continued its journey.

"There's wankers who can put an album together in their sodding bedrooms," continued Donovan. "Then the tossers sell the poxy thing on the internet while they're lying in bed. Like I said, it's all about technology these days, your actual musical talent's a distant second."

More tugs on his nose.

"Record companies like us are getting shafted right and left. And then, when I do take a chance on some up-and-comer, they turn around and kick me in the bollocks. I mean, look at Kelly Anton."

Frank felt his old paparazzo antenna spring up. He stiffened like a hound that's caught a scent.

"You trying to tell me you signed Kelly Anton?" he asked.

For the twenty years before his conviction, ten either side of the millennium — the golden age of paparazzi, according to Frank — his photos of the rich and famous ran in every gossip sheet and celebrity rag in Britain, Europe, and the U.S. There was no way Frank could stifle the opportunistic reactions of a seasoned pap despite the ban on his working as one — a condition of his suspended sentence.

In his glory days as a paparazzo he'd been unbeatable at sniffing out a celebrity's antics before they even happened.

But since his conviction Frank had tried to avoid any tittle tattle of the glitterati's fuck-ups. Hearing about photo opportunities that would once have earned him thousands but were now out of bounds was only likely to send him headlong into a bottle. However, Frank couldn't help but be aware of the sensational success of Kelly Anton's first album. The fact that it had been a massive hit and won music awards on both sides of the Atlantic was all over the news, not to mention her face plastered on billboards and posters across London. A record-company executive with Kelly Anton in his stable of artists would certainly have the means to provide for a spouse.

"Uncle Alf did a concert a couple of years ago where she was the opening act," said Donovan. "Before she was anybody much, obviously. She wanted so many sound checks Alf nearly lost his rag. Turns out she was all over 'im after it was all sorted, best sound she's ever 'ad. Well, Alf knows a thing or two, doesn't he? He's worked with the greats. Anyway, Alf's telling me how he reckons she's got what it takes, and then some, and how she was bitching to him about how no record company will look at her. When Alf told me all this, I was on it like a rat up a drainpipe, wasn't I?"

More like a ferret, thought Frank. He couldn't bear to look at Donovan's freckled face a moment longer. He gazed through grease-smeared glass at the misty underbelly of cloud cover that swathed the top floors of one of the new blocks of luxury flats that lined Queenstown Road. He thought about Donovan's tale of good fortune. The fact that his son-in-law's expression portrayed not an iota of smugness annoyed Frank more than if Donovan had been chortling with self-congratulation. It was his apparent lack of appreciation for his jammy situation that was so irritating to Frank, who was painfully aware that he'd been exactly the same, when he was earning a packet as a paparazzo — oblivious of the fact he was leading a charmed life, never imagining it could end in ignominy.

"Well, I'm glad for Whitney's sake," muttered Frank, venturing a look at his son-in-law.

"Thanks, Frank, that's really big of you."

Another yank on the nose. Maybe Donovan was more nervous than Frank had thought.

"It hasn't been a complete doddle though. For the first few months, while Kelly was cutting the album, and then when it was so well received, it was all sunshine and roses. But ever since then — for the last twelve friggin' months — not only has she done sod-all, she's been out of her head 24/7."

Frank had heard rumours about drugs and stories of collapses on stage. In his paparazzo days he'd have sniffed out every sordid episode in Kelly Anton's life before it broke, but these days he steered well away from any situation where he may discover destructive dross in a celebrity's life. He had enough trouble keeping his own demons at bay.

"I'm trying as hard as I can though, Frank. Take tonight, for example. At great expense to management I've fixed up a gig for her at a club in Vauxhall, to try and kick start the creative process. Supposedly she's going to try out some new material. The punters don't know she's going to be there, they'll go into cardiac arrest when Kelly Anton walks on stage right after the bunch of lame hip-hoppers they've paid a measly few quid to see."

Frank turned his head away. Since giving up the demon drink he'd sometimes been caught unawares by an unaccustomed empathy for others' dodgy predicaments. It had been so strong on occasion that he'd shed a tear or two, wondering what the hell was wrong with him. His eyes were dry, but he was surprised to find himself not unsympathetic to Donovan's obvious frustration with his broody golden goose, in the form of a recording star too fucked-up to produce the goods. Frank had seen enough of them to know that their story invariably ended in tragedy for all involved.

"Mind you, the club crowd will have guessed something's going on," said Donovan. "Kelly wants all mobiles held at the door, if you can believe it. She don't want no pirate videos all over the net, made on fancy new smart phones, in case her new stuff turns out to be rubbish."

The bus was trundling across Chelsea Bridge. Frank stared at a rusting supermarket trolley half submerged in an expanse of mud bordering the river. He wondered how long Donovan — and by association, Whitney — could stay solvent without the income that a star like Kelly Anton must provide him.

"I can't let the press know, obviously — Kelly'd have a shit fit," said Donovan.

At the mention of a lack of media presence Frank quickly turned his attention from the view of the turbid Thames to scrutinize Donovan's face.

"It took some coaxing, Frank. But I fed her the line that she needs to get back to her roots — try and recapture some of the freshness. It's a long shot, I know, but desperate times call for desperate measures, yeah? They're going to close the doors just before she goes on and she's supposed to do one set and then leg it. I just pray she's not off her box on something or other."

More nose tugs. The skin beginning to turn pink.

"If she's that screwed up, how do you know she'll show?" asked Frank.

"Oh, she'll show alright. Kelly's a ginormous diva. Apart from the coke and the crack, she's an adoration junkie. Well, I tell you Frank, the adoration is in danger of turning to disgust, which is the kiss of death. Nobody wants nothing to do with a strung-out singer who can't hack it no more."

The bus trundled into Chelsea Bridge Road. Donovan slid out of his seat and stooped to peer, like a startled rodent, out of the window to check the bus's location.

"This is me, Frank."

He thrust out a hand. There would have been a time when there was no way Frank was going to shake it. But, with the A.A. Twelve Step programme playing on his conscience, Frank thought that perhaps it was time to start making amends to Donovan — and therefore Whitney — for whatever the hell it was he'd done to hurt them. But then Frank realized Donovan wasn't expecting a handshake but was presenting him with a small piece of canary yellow paper printed in garish purple ink.

"Here's my contact info., Frank. If there's ever anything you need or I can do, don't even hesitate, alright?"

Frank took the business card and held it gingerly between thumb and fingertip. Donovan bolted down the stairs before Frank could come up with a message for his daughter. Probably just as well, he said to himself. A saying of his mother's floated into his head that was the direct opposite of the A.A. creed: 'Least said, soonest mended.'. If only it were true, Frank thought.

He watched out of the window as Donovan slithered off the bus in front of other departing passengers. As the bus pulled away Frank glimpsed his son-in-law hail a vacant cab that must have been idling behind the bus. He wondered why Donovan hadn't taken a taxi in the first place. Buses weren't his style, and expense was obviously not an issue.

Frank gazed at the bright yellow business card. He considered how, if any pap got wind of Kelly's gig in Vauxhall and popped some shots, they'd make a mint. He knew full well that exclusive photos of Kelly Anton would be worth a fortune, no matter what condition she was in.

WHEN KELLY ANTON woke up, her first thought was that at least the sodding sun didn't appear to be out. Sunny mornings were one of the increasing number of occasions when she kicked herself for not resisting Donovan, when he'd insisted that she should buy an open-plan penthouse, with its soaring wall of glass facing east and north. Kelly would be eternally grateful to Donovan for taking a flyer on her and her music when nobody else would, but Jesus, he was stubborn. Once he had an idea in his head, he was like a dog with a bone, the harder you tried to get him to drop it, the more he gnawed away at it. When she tried to claim she couldn't afford to buy the place, Donovan had scoffed. "Of course you can, you just won a fistful of BRIT awards and a shedload of Grammys. You're a bloody superstar, and superstars don't live with their parents in a terraced house in Battersea, for fuck's sake." In the end she'd agreed to buy the penthouse more to keep him quiet than anything else.

When Kelly summoned up the courage to open her eyes, she squinted at a one-hundred-and-eighty-degree expanse of leaden London sky that made her wish she'd kept her lids closed. She couldn't win: if the sun was out it blinded her, and cloudy mornings weighed her down.

Kelly rolled onto her side and groped for the reassurance of Jason's warm skin. Her fingers, with chipped nail varnish the colour of blood blisters, fluttered tentatively in the air above his naked back and then rested, butterfly fashion, on a shoulder blade. Jason groaned and made a feeble attempt to wriggle out of reach. Kelly, undeterred, traced an exploratory path down the side of his body, fingertips moving tentatively from one rib to the next, as though trying to read his mood from contours of bone separated by valleys of muscle. After being together for more than a year, Kelly wasn't entirely sure that she had Jason pegged.

Before she met him, Kelly had always assumed everybody was more or less the same. But hanging out with Jason — or to use his full title, the Honourable Jason Ramsay Campbell — and his crowd, who all seemed to go by three names, she realized that some people were less the same than others. And, with his public-school education, his family's three houses dotted around the world, and his flat in Kensington, Jason was a lot different from her Battersea friends, her family, and everybody else she knew.

She'd met him at one of her regular gigs at the Cobden Club, just before her album was released. Nobody but a few club regulars knew who she was back then. As she began her act that night, she'd noticed him and his crowd in the audience. Nobody could have missed their posh braying, it almost drowned out her intro music. What they were doing, slumming it north of the Westway, far from their usual tony haunts, God only knew. She stood at the mike, hoping somebody would tell them to put a lid on it, when Jason, who, she noticed, had been the only one of them paying her any attention, loudly told the rest of them to "shut the fuck up." She put her hands together and bowed her head in his direction, like some kind of Indian princess. Although Jason was a few yards from the stage, and even though his smile wasn't the broadest, his vibe of confidence and self-assurance was obvious to her. Kelly might normally have bridled against the sense of privilege he gave off, but knowing he was on her side, she was more reassured than repulsed. She'd sung better than usual that night, looking at Jason most of the time. She told herself she often zeroed in on an audience member, believing she gave the song more feeling if she focussed on someone in particular. But she had to admit, Jason was easy on the eyes, and she'd always been a sucker for auburn hair, especially when it was stylishly unkempt, like Jason's. When she finished, he'd come right up to the stage and asked her if she'd have a drink with him. A day or so later — during which time they'd barely left the flat he shared with his best mate, Jonny — her album came out and immediately started climbing the charts. It seemed like Jason had been her lucky charm. She thought she'd better hold on to him. Not that she had any inclination to let go of him, she'd never been so turned on by a guy as by Jason.

She loved his long body with a barely discernible waist and his surprisingly robust, hairy legs. She'd never seen Jason move awkwardly, not even when he was drunk, or high. He always moved gracefully. Not in a poncey way, like some of the other poshos in his upper-class crowd, but fluidly, like an otter. Not that Kelly could remember having met an otter, but her mother, Ruth, had read a book to her when she was a kid about a man who kept otters in the wilds of Scotland. Ruth was a magical reader who infused such life into the passages that little Kelly had no trouble imagining every scene. Even when Jason wasn't drunk or high, there was a languor in his mannerisms and in his speech, which mesmerized Kelly from the get-go. Her socialist mother claimed — disapprovingly — it was an entitled, public-schoolboy thing, but that and his take-no-shit attitude were the clinchers for Kelly.

Kelly had cursed Google up and down when her mother did some digging and found out that one of Jason's ancestors was a slave owner.

"When you mentioned his family was Scottish, I remembered that lots of the plantations in Jamaica used to be owned by Scots," Ruth had said. "And sure enough, the Campbells were in there with a sugar plantation."

"For Christ's sake, Mum, you can't blame Jason for that.

Shake any of them old family trees and a shady character will fall out."

But her mother wouldn't drop it.

"Slaves were given their owner's family name, so these days every second person on the island has a Scottish surname," Ruth had said. "There's loads of Campbells. For all we know Jason's family might have owned your father's great-grandparents."

"But our name isn't Campbell, is it? So, I think Jason's off the hook."

"All I'm saying is their wealth is suspect. And, like it or not, your boyfriend may well be living the life of Riley as a direct result of your ancestors' slavery."

Kelly didn't appreciate her mother's suspicions and theories. They made her wonder whether Jason had ever treated her as some kind of inferior. But she came to the conclusion that he'd never done any such thing. He was certainly no racist. He claimed to like her Jamaican father — despite his obvious distrust of Jason — on the few occasions they'd met. And Jason had never mansplained anything to her. In fact, she could think of more than one occasion when he asked her to tell him things, like how she worked with the producer on her album, or about the difference between playing guitar and piano when she was performing. He even asked her once what it was like, growing up in South London as a mixed-race kid.

If she ever had any niggles of worry, Kelly knew they were more about her own hang-ups rather than because of anything Jason might say or do. As much as Jason's undisputed cool impressed her, it also scared her slightly. Kelly sometimes wondered, were he to decide she wasn't the flavour of the month, how long he'd stick around.

Kelly couldn't keep her eyes closed any longer. She was pleased to see that the clouds had thinned, and the weather was brightening. But then she remembered the gig Donovan had arranged for her that evening. As if she'd be inspired by a poxy club in Vauxhall, for fuck's sake. It was all part of his mental plan to make the best use of her 'drought,' as he called her recent lack of material. She supposed she ought to be grateful to Donovan for not ditching her when she'd come up with her 'songwriter's block' excuse. But, as Jason put it, "What are the chances of him signing another multiplatinum artist? Of course he's going to wait it out."

Nevertheless, Donovan being Donovan, he couldn't just leave it at that. Especially after she got masses of tabloid press when some paps snapped her and Jason, looking a bit rough, coming out of a club. It wasn't only the rubbish media at home that covered it, but MTV and TMZ in America were all over it too. Kelly was appalled when they described her as being high as a kite. Admittedly Jason had done a little crack that night, but Kelly never touched the stuff, or any other drug come to that. She liked to think she was always sorted. The thought that she might be out of control scared the shit out of her. When some toe-rag paparazzo had snapped the photo, she'd just been dog tired and had drunk two barley wines, one over her normal limit. The shit clothes she was wearing at the time hadn't helped either. But over the week or so of the massive press coverage — as much or more attention than winning her sodding awards — her sales increased substantially. That's when Donovan had come up with his bonkers scheme of making out the delay on her second album was because she was trashed with drugs.

"It'll give you as much time as you want — within reason — and it'll keep your name on punters' lips," he'd said.

"And what about my frigging reputation?" she'd said. "Not to mention what my parents will think."

"It'll only be for a while to give you a chance to get some stuff together," he wheedled. "Then we can claim you've cleaned up your act. You'll be adored and admired for going through the rehab thing, and the new album will get more attention because of all the vultures circling around hoping it's shite."

Kelly thought it was a crap way to keep up the spin, never mind that old saying about there being 'no such thing as bad publicity.' If she'd known Donovan's dumb idea would make matters so much worse, she'd never have gone along with it. As it was, she'd fought like fuck against it, but Donovan leant on her so heavily, and there was no way she was going to explain to him the real reason for her lack of material. She'd caved, just as she'd given in when he cajoled her into buying the penthouse. She thought it might cause more problems with her father, but she'd never dreamt he'd react as badly as he did. She'd been stupid when she made matters worse by yelling at her father that, even if it were true, occasional crack was no worse than his ganja habit. After that — and the way Donovan pushed her to sometimes act the part in public — there was no way he'd believe she wasn't touching the stuff.

And then, as her feelings for Jason intensified, she'd felt guilty for getting him involved, but was too afraid of losing him to tell him exactly what was going on.

"Can you believe this shit?" Jason had once said about a particularly vicious article in the Mail after she'd laid it on a bit, roughing herself up in the Ladies before staggering out of the club they'd been in. "We ought to sue the bastards."

"I don't advise it, given your habit," she'd said. The minute the words were out of her mouth she regretted them — Jason wasn't hard-core, he just enjoyed a bit of crack occasionally. But she'd panicked, and he was a user nonetheless. He'd been somewhat under the influence on the night in question.

"Being smeared by the gutter press is what happens

when you sleep with a sexy superstar," Kelly had quickly said, trying to make a joke of it.

Donovan was the same pushy bugger about the 'drought' ruse as he'd been pushing her to buy the penthouse. At least she'd been strong when he first went on about her buying a house in Kensington or Holland Park. "It's an image thing," he's said. But she'd put her foot down, insisting she wanted to stay south of the river. She'd lived in Battersea all her life, hadn't she? Why the hell would she want to rattle around in one of those monstrous old places up near Notting Hill?

Donovan capitulated, but, being a persistent little prick, he'd sat her down and showed her the web site for a riverside building not far from where she'd grown up. It sat on the south bank slap bang between the Battersea and Albert bridges, with a massive golf-ball-shaped behind that Kelly thought was hideous. Donovan tried to make out it was beautiful.

"Look what it says," he said. "'From behind, dotted with windows and recessed balconies, it looks like a musical score.' It's like it was made for you."

Despite Kelly's misgivings she realized it was within walking distance of her parents' house, where she'd grown up. Jason liked the look of the penthouse, and she had to admit she thought buying it would put her on more of a par with his friends. Not that she cared much about his crowd, but she wanted to keep Jason sweet. However, the main deciding wow-factor for Kelly was a residents' swimming pool. Before the 'drought', she'd come up with all her best music while swimming. Melodies came easily when she had her head in the water.

Her father, who, like most Jamaicans, had never learnt to swim, was perplexed by the amount of time she spent at the local swimming pool as a kid. Kelly's mother, born and brought up in Birmingham, often teased him.

"How can you not know how to swim? You grew up on a little island."

"Jamaica not so little. And water for washin' 'n' fishin', not for playin' in."

When she was swimming Kelly's mind seemed to dip and dive dolphin-style alongside her, completely unfettered and separated from her body. When she started coming up with melodies, musical notes darted like schools of tropical fish, until they assumed a specific order to match the words she'd memorized. Afterwards, in the Latchmere Leisure Centre changing room, before anyone knew who she was, she'd furiously scribbled complete melodies into a dog-eared notebook, panicked that she'd forget if she didn't immediately commit them to ink on paper after her swim. Once or twice she'd let out a hoot of delight that she'd managed to come up with a perfect arrangement of notes. Other women, assuming she was on something, hastily finished dressing and legged it out of the changing room as fast as they could.

So, Kelly had said, 'Go on then,' to Donovan about plonking four million pounds down, as casually as if she was down the pub agreeing to buy a barley wine, her usual tipple, rather than shelling out buckets-full of cash for a posh riverside apartment.

It turned out the swimming pool in her building had proved a dud when it came to writing lyrics. It was like a mausoleum. Deserted, pristine, and silent, it creeped her out. She persevered — God knows she tried. But the words simply evaded her.

She wondered if the tumultuous atmosphere of the Latchmere pool where she'd composed her best melodies would be better. Kids screaming, swimming instructors bellowing. Old men doggy paddling and large ladies enjoying a stately breaststroke in the slow lane next to hers. But she'd be spotted within seconds. Before she could swim a lap, the place would be chock-a-block with ferocious fans and ravening paps. She could just imagine the scrum in the changing room. Everybody with their new smart phones with built-in cameras, all jostling to get a shot of Kelly Anton in the altogether.

In the last couple of weeks she'd managed to squeeze out a verse or two of corny lyrics. Once she had some words, the music came easily enough, so maybe the pool in her building wasn't a complete waste. Donovan had insisted she try them out in front of an audience. And if she bombed in the dump he'd booked her into, nobody would know or really give a shit. The club had resisted, kicking and screaming, her demand that all mobiles — especially the new ones that could shoot videos — be handed in at the door. But she'd put her foot down. No shitty amateur clips on YouTube, thank you very much. They patted everyone down and looked in every bag for weapons anyway. How much of a problem could it be? In the end Donovan told her he'd slipped them a couple of grand for their trouble. And she'd laid it on the line — absolutely no press.

Vauxhall for fuck's sake! What would he come up with next?

"ALRIGHT, ALI?" SAID Frank as cheerily as he could, which wasn't a bad effort given the torture of his present situation. The devil on his shoulder, the one that constantly tried to prod Frank into having a drink — just one drink, what could be the harm? — had embarked on a new project. It reminded him every minute of the half-hour since Donovan had left Frank on the bus about his hot-shit-record-company-executive son-in-law's claim of exclusion of media at Kelly Anton's gig. Frank knew that any one of the newspapers and magazines where he used to sell photos would pay the equivalent of three months of his present wages for a single, exclusive photograph of the super star on stage.

"Uh uh," grunted Ali, shoulders hunched, his head held, resolute, twelve inches from his monitor. Frank sat at his desk, moved his mouse to wake up his computer, and glanced across at the slight twenty-two-year-old. Ali's gleaming skin was flushed with vermilion from the reflected colours of a bunch of tomatoes that filled his screen. Frank could see that he was painstakingly removing and retouching blemishes on their surface, so they'd appear even more luscious. The young Photoshop hotshot had been introduced to Frank as 'I.T. Ali,' at the photo agency where Frank finally found a job, on the strength of a tip-off from a sympathetic ex-client, one of the many photo editors Frank had supplied with photos over the years.

Frank's days at FoodFoto Ltd., the largest bank of food photography in Britain, were mostly taken up with the simple but tedious work of cross-referencing and backing up digital files. He thought he'd misheard when they told him how low his salary would be. The dosh he'd shelled out every week on parking fines alone when he worked as a paparazzo was more than the total they were offering him for a week's work at FoodFoto. But it was better than nothing, which is what he was earning at the time.

Frank had soon discovered that Ali's information technology moniker was coined to differentiate him from 'Bean Counter Ali,' the company accountant. It was just as well that Frank wasn't offended by Ali's apparent indifference to him since they shared cramped quarters in what was once the coal cellar of the Pimlico terraced house that accommodated the agency. Ali was sometimes summoned to the offices upstairs to address computer issues, but mostly he and Frank spent their working hours together in the confines of the ten by nine metre — hundred square feet to Frank, who hadn't quite made the leap to metric — windowless room in the bowels of the old building.

When he was first shown the dimly lit cell of a room where he'd be working for eight hours a day, five days a week, Frank was seriously considering doing a runner. He may have been on his uppers, but did he really need to live like a fucking mole for eight hours a day, five days a week? It was bad enough he was reduced to living in a dingy bedsit/studio apartment. Frank had been sorely tempted to head for the nearest pub in disgust, when Ali casually mentioned a system of hard drives that he'd set up to accommodate more than a million photographs, all stored in the confines of a couple of other small basement rooms. Frank realized that toiling alongside the computer nerd could provide the lifeline he'd been praying for. He took the job on the spot.

Frank's problem — and he hoped his salvation — was that before everything went pear-shaped and he lost his company, he hadn't had time to get his booze-soaked head around the idea that he should have all his older non-digital stock scanned. His collection was golden. Potential income ran into the hundreds of thousands of pounds, but only if photos could be displayed and transmitted digitally. The total sum of his negatives, prints, and transparencies were crammed into fire-proof metal filing cabinets that filled at least twenty times the space taken up by Ali's compact system of hard drives even though Frank's collection was a tenth the size of FoodFoto's vast inventory.

Somehow Frank had pulled himself together enough during his last days of solvency to cajole a couple of ex-employees to help him rustle all the filing cabinets out of his building and into a storage unit before the bailiffs arrived.

He couldn't believe his luck when neither Christine nor her lawyers realized the value of his old shots — not only the massive amount of celebrity material but also the hundreds of photos taken during Frank's stint as a press photographer at the Mail. As a result, the collection hadn't come into play in his divorce settlement. Not that there was much left after the bankruptcy. The bank took the house in Notting Hill, and the other creditors took everything else. What little that was left, Christine took. Frank was particularly bitter that she'd even grabbed all the family photo albums he'd spent hours organizing, not to mention his five hundred or more vinyl records.

Any guilty thoughts Frank may have had about concealing the worth of his photography stock were dispelled when he was forced to spend every night for six months in his storage unit, curled up in an old sleeping bag, a flimsy piece of foam the only buffer between him and a concrete floor. He'd been so broke that every penny of the small sum he'd managed to hold on to went toward the storage unit's rental, with the odd pound or two left over for an occasional bottle of gut-rot sherry or port. Frank had come close to peddling some of the material he'd amassed over almost thirty years, but he always knew it'd be difficult to unload random analog material — a photoprint here or a transparency there. He could try and sell off his complete collection as it stood to an established photo agency, but even at his worst moments, when the booze might have shaken his resolve, he resisted, knowing he'd only make a fraction of its potential worth.

So, Frank held on in his storage unit for the day when he could afford to convert the whole shebang into digitized images. It was typical of his recent bad luck that the winter turned out to be particularly brassy. Frank had an idea how breeze blocks earned their name — a brisk draught whipping through walls made of the frigging things had frozen his balls off for months. The day after his meagre nest egg was completely spent, he managed to find work as a foot messenger with a courier company. As well as the cost of the rental unit, the job paid enough for a dormitory bed in a hostel. There he was introduced to Alcoholics Anonymous and swore off the booze.

When he met Ali, Frank made up his mind to make the diminutive computer-nerd his guardian angel. He planned to learn everything he needed to know from Ali ready for the day when he could buy a high-end scanner and the rest of the equipment he'd need. Then he could start using the skills he'd learnt from Ali to cash in on the untold value of his creaking metal filing cabinets stuffed with negatives, prints and transparencies. Maybe then he could get back to earning the kind of money he used to pull, and — more importantly — perhaps his daughter would let him back into her life.

"You've probably heard of Kelly Anton, right?" Frank asked Ali, for two reasons. Firstly, because he knew he'd get a rise out of the nineteen-year-old. And secondly, because he just couldn't shift the devil on his shoulder prodding him about Kelly's gig.

"I live in Kennington, not Karachi," muttered Ali.

"What do you think?" asked Frank.

"Of Kelly Anton or your sad question?"

Despite, or maybe because of, his cool confidence, Frank liked Ali. Most young people with his smarts would be falling over themselves to show the world how much they knew. But Ali couldn't be arsed.

"Well, it's obvious what you think of my question, so why don't you enlighten me with your thoughts on Kelly Anton," said Frank.

He was pleased when Ali pushed his chair away from his monitor and sat back. Frank nagged Ali as much as he thought he could without being overly paternal about the boy's bad posture and about him not stretching regularly. It wasn't Frank's ageing generation that was destined to bring down the National Health Service as people seemed to fear. It would be the millions of young people like Ali who'd be stricken in their maturity with carpal tunnel syndrome and chronic arthritis from sitting hunched over a computer screen all day long. Not to mention failing eyesight. Frank often wondered how the country would support such a vast population of blind, crippled, computer veterans.

"Kelly Anton is sick," pronounced Ali. "Not just a brilliant musician, but a great songwriter, and a fantastic voice."

Frank could always tell when Ali was into something, because the young techno geek didn't bother to take the piss. He just weighed in and explained things, as though he was worldly wise and Frank the naïve innocent.

"Haven't you never seen her?" Ali asked.

"Just the odd photo, not actually performing," said Frank.

Ali turned purposefully to his computer, hid the tomatoes on his screen with a deft keyboard command and opened his server. It was clear he was going to search for Kelly Anton.

"What about Bertie Big Bollocks?" said Frank, referring to their boss, Robert Smedley, as Ali double-clicked on a YouTube icon. "His office is right over our heads."

"With these poor excuse for speakers he won't hear much," said Ali. "And when was the last time he sank to our level? But on the off chance that he does grant us the pleasure of his company, we're doing a Final Cut Pro on-line seminar, all right? That'll please him. He's always on to me about 'exploring video.' As if we don't have anything else to do."

For all his reticence Ali could sometimes be extremely camp. He gave his last sentence a dramatic emphasis that would have been the envy of any drag queen. Frank once overheard Cheryl, the receptionist, refer to him as 'Batty Boy Ali.' He supposed she could have been talking about the company accountant, 'Bean Counter Ali,' but it seemed unlikely. The fifty-something-year-old number cruncher was as hetero as they come. Photos of his seven kids were strewn around his cubicle like testaments to his testosterone — grinning white-toothed evidence of his virility.

Before Ali had double-clicked on the YouTube icon, Frank noticed the number of videos available in response to Ali's search for 'kelly anton performances.' Five hundred and seventy-six! Frank wasn't in the habit of looking up videos of recording artists, but it sounded like a hell of a lot to him. But then, as they waited for the live area to load, Frank noticed the number of hits for that particular video.

"A hundred and twenty million frigging views?" Frank exclaimed. He couldn't believe his eyes.

"Ye-ah!" declared Ali, emphasizing the word as if he were confirming the potency of social media to a mentally challenged Neanderthal.

The video-screen area of Ali's monitor cleared to reveal the reclining figure of a light-skinned black woman. Frank reckoned she must be around his daughter's, Whitney's, age, twenty-six or so. She was dressed in a loose turquoise shirt-style dress, buttons undone to reveal the top of a skimpy bra. Her tousled tresses trembled as she began to sing. The camera zoomed slowly to fill the frame with her face. Pink lip gloss caught the light as she opened her mouth.

Kelly's voice caused Frank's scalp to tighten and he felt the hairs on the back of his neck bristle. Not in a million years would he have expected such a mature bluesy sound — smoky, but strong and potent, with a deep fully-rounded tone. It matched the world-worn quality in her eyes, which was accentuated by the retro style of her generous eyeliner. As the song unwound, Kelly sat up and hugged her bony knees, the body language of an uneasy child rather than of the resolute woman her voice suggested. Some notes had a cracked raw quality that, together with a thick silver eyebrow ring and a tattooed snake slithering across her chest, leant Kelly a hard-ass demeanour. What a frigging voice, Frank thought. Billie Holiday, Nina Simone, Aretha Franklin — all came to mind but none of them really fit. An asset like her didn't fall into a record company's lap more than once or twice in a lifetime. No wonder Donovan had his knickers in a twist that she wasn't producing the goods for a new album.

"Play it again," demanded Frank, as soon as the song ended, and the screen went abruptly to black. "I want to listen to the words."

"Yes, sahib. Right away at once, sahib," said Ali in an exaggerated Pakistani accent, which he adopted if Frank ever sounded remotely as if he was ordering the lad around.

Frank tried his best to follow the words, but he was sidetracked by thoughts of how terrifically sad the song made him feel, not just from the couple of lines he could comprehend but the combination of wounded vulnerability peppered with occasional flashes of aggression that Kelly's voice managed to communicate.

"I couldn't catch all of that," Frank confessed, when the song ended for the second time.

"Well you wouldn't, would you?" said Ali, but more in a sympathetic tone rather than his sometimes-starchy manner. Perhaps he'd sussed how affected Frank was by the song.

"Here," Ali said. He punched 'kelly anton song lyrics' into the search engine, clicked on a link, then on the song's title. Frank read the three verses that popped up on Ali's screen.

It's Like I'm Outside

The night draws down
Rude girl out on the town
Living it large in the bar
It's like I'm outside
Just watching her ride

The evening drags out
Bile flush in her mout(h)
As pain and misery mount
Her face don't even crack
She's mastered the knack

She's fake and she's snide
But she can't turn the tide
And now she can't love her
Herself nor no other
Just a girl in a bar
Struggling not to be smother
And it's like she's outside
Just watching the ride

Ali scrolled down to reveal the rest of the lyrics, but Frank had had enough. He rolled back to his computer and opened the agency's FTP site. He started downloading some files that had arrived from a photographer overnight.

"Told you she was brilliant, didn't I?" said Ali.

"Mmmm," muttered Frank. It wasn't lost on him that their roles were reversed. Frank, usually the instigator of discussion, was playing the evasive partner to Ali's probing.

"Well, did you like it?" pressed Ali, obviously frustrated by Frank's lack of a response.

"Like you say, she's brilliant," conceded Frank, staring at the Fetch software dog galloping in place to indicate the copying of a file onto his hard drive. He hoped his simple statement would put an end to their conversation. There was no way on God's earth he was going to explain to Ali that the song had touched a massive nerve. How many nights, or days come to that, had Frank experienced the sensation that Kelly hinted at? A distinct impression that he was standing outside himself, watching as he was thrown around on some wild ride that he couldn't stop. As if aboard an endless fairground attraction, or astride a demented run-away stallion, over which he had absolutely no control. Drink after drink after drink after drink. The worst part had been the feeling of absolute certainty that it would all end badly — as it had. That he'd eventually be 'smother' as Kelly phrased it — as he had been.

And if the young singer was saying what Frank thought she was saying about bogus bravado and the self-loathing it generates, then he had no idea how someone in their early twenties could have had the kind of bleak experiences that led to such a self-destructive trajectory. He shuddered to think that Kelly might have actually experienced the desolation that the words of the song suggested. What made it all so much more gut-wrenching was the angry and confrontational heartbreak in her voice. Christ knows how much more affected he'd be if he heard her on decent quality speakers.

What a morning! First Donovan and now this. Frank couldn't hold back a wry smile when the thought occurred to him that it was enough to drive a person to drink.

"Most of those performance videos are a year or so old." Ali had returned to tweaking his tomatoes, but clearly felt that his dexterity allowed him to retouch and talk at the same time. "As far as I know she hasn't done much lately except take drugs and hang out with her useless prat of a boyfriend. There's a couple of videos of them completely trashed if you want to see."

"I've seen enough," said Frank. "And anyway, Bertie Big Bollocks will be wondering why these files haven't been downloaded and sorted if I don't get on with it."

For ten or fifteen minutes the only sounds were the clicking of Frank and Ali's mice and the distant rumble of London traffic interspersed with the sound of floorboards creaking as Robert Smedley moved around in his office above them.

JASON LAY NAKED on his stomach, a wrinkled sheet covering only his feet and calves. Kelly moved her hand from his ribs to half-heartedly stroke his bum, less because she was horny and more as a distraction from thoughts of that evening's gig. Why Donovan had picked Vauxhall, Christ only knew. All he'd told her was the place was under some railway arches — not exactly inspiring. Christ knows how she'd managed to come up with some lyrics that weren't totally useless. Only the one song though. She just hoped to fuck the crowd would be so pumped to see her she could get by with doing mostly old stuff. She distractedly drummed her fingers on Jason's backside. He tensed and relaxed his buttocks a couple of times in quick succession, like an animal twitching its flanks to dislodge an irritating fly. Undaunted, Kelly continued to stroke his skin with her fingertips. She always found Jason's arse surprisingly smooth, given the hairiness of his thighs and crotch. Now, when she cupped one of his cheeks in her hand and lightly squeezed, he let out a muffled moan of protest, his face buried in his pillow. But at the same time, he spread his legs slightly. Jason had been an exciting lover from the get-go, mainly because she'd given him room, permission — whatever — to shed the few inhibitions he'd had when they met. Or maybe it was that she encouraged him to be more imaginative. Whichever, Kelly knew that, despite his complaining whimper, Jason's move was probably an appeal for her to continue the foreplay she knew he liked.

When they first started hanging out, she imagined that Jason disapproved of her suggestions. Not the sexual kind — he was always eager — but other things. If she came up with a new place to eat, an act to see, or an unusual drink, Jason would often say "Really?" She took his tone to mean he was sceptical her idea was any good, so she felt she had to justify herself. Kelly supposed the process would annoy the shit out of most people, but she went along with it. She liked to think that having to defend her choices made her more discriminating. But the longer they were together — Jason more or less lived at the penthouse after she'd bought it — Kelly began to realize his questioning of her suggestions came from the restricted life he'd led until he met her. She soon learnt that his experiences had been confined to an amazingly few places and activities that he and his crowd, and perhaps their parents too, had always frequented or done. She came to understand that he wasn't so much doubting Kelly's suggestions as expressing wonder about them. He'd never said as much, but Kelly realized she was broadening his horizons.

Jason still had his face pressed to the pillow, motionless but for the slight rise and fall of his ribcage. But then he sighed loudly and pushed his crotch into the mattress, spreading his thighs an inch or so more. Should she take up the gauntlet, if that's what it was? Hell, why not? There was sod-all else to do before the evening's gig. She moved her hand down and stroked the line of hair between his legs, springy as spun wire. She tugged it gently, then probed the hair to gently massage the area immediately behind his balls, letting her fingernails occasionally brush the back of his scrotum in the process. Jason shifted his hips slightly, increasing the pressure on her fingers. He turned his head free of his pillow so he could moan, a deep-throated expression of pleasure.

Bingo! The surge of power Kelly experienced was always a turn on. And now that Jason was genuinely aroused, her breathing deepened at the prospect of sex with him. At this point she often thought of the lyrics to an old Dory Previn track her father used to play about a woman describing two lovers — "one would make love, and the other would fuck." With Jason she had both men rolled into one. As a love-maker he had the astonishing ability to keep her hovering deliciously on the edge until, just as she thought she'd surge over, he'd retreat and concentrate on a lesser erogenous zone, and the process would start all over again. Each time involved more torment than the last until, when he did eventually bring her to climax, her orgasm was more body shattering than she could have imagined. Then he would fuck her.

In one of their mother/daughter evenings down the pub — before fame put a stop to outings to the local — Ruth had once confided to Kelly that she "liked a good pounding now and again." And that's exactly what Jason supplied. Which Kelly almost always enjoyed, despite wondering on occasion about the sadist in Jason. And what about herself? Did she experience a masochistic thrill not knowing for sure whether he'd stop even if she begged? They didn't have anything as conventional as a safe word, but she was sure that, if she insisted, he'd back off.

Without claiming it as something she'd experienced, she brought up with her Dad the sensation of losing control and/or caution during lovemaking, in the hope that a song would ensue. But he'd wrinkled his nose as if he smelt something rotten. She'd often talked to him about other intimate aspects of her relationships as a stimulus for songs, but never so explicitly about sex. She supposed it was a step too far.

Any thoughts she may have had of her father were banished when Jason shifted onto his side, lifted an arm, and slowly traced a line with his fingers from her belly button to her clitoris, where he lingered, making a low, closemouthed murmur of appreciation. The thing Kelly loved about being a musician was that she had all day before a gig to just hang out. And Jason had nowhere he had to be.

There'd been chit chat about him starting a business with Jonny, full name Jonathon Lachlan Abernathy. He and Jason had known each other since they were born. It seemed to Kelly — the way they talked — that their families together must own half of Scotland. And they both went to the same posh school that they were always dissing. If she ever thought about it, she assumed that private schools would have brilliant teachers, but to hear Jason and Jonny talk, she had the impression all of theirs were crap. Her school, John Paul II in Wandsworth, hadn't been great either, but Ruth had pushed for the school because of its lively music programme. Kelly's father's prejudices against organized religion and his initial mutterings about "dem rass catlicks" were silenced once he heard that Kelly would have free after-school music lessons.

Jason and Jonny were always talking about making documentaries, something Jason knew a bit about from his part-time job at a production company. She knew that Jason wasn't working that day, so — like her — was in no rush to get out of bed.

"I'M SURPRISED you don't want to see Kelly Anton trashed out of her head," said Ali. "I'd have thought you'd have been into that stuff, being a 'paparazzo.'" His sneery comment — with accompanying air quotes — shattered the peaceful atmosphere of their basement office.

Frank sighed inwardly, recognizing the disapproval in his young workmate's exaggeratedly disdainful pronunciation of the word paparazzo. Frank had no idea how Ali had discovered his past profession, maybe Bertie Big Bollocks had mentioned it and word had got around. Ali had tried jerking Frank's chain about having been a paparazzo a couple of times before, but Frank had managed to ignore him.

Early in his career as a photographer of the rich and famous Frank had often argued passionately in defence of his means of earning a living. But he soon learned that there was little point. People who had no first-hand experience of celebrities or of the celebrity/photographer relationship simply couldn't understand the complexity of the situation. Most viewed paparazzi as simply scum of the earth, particularly since the death of Princess Diana.

"I'm not a paparazzo anymore," said Frank.

"Just as well," muttered Ali. "Blood-sucking leeches."

"Whatever," said Frank, trying to sound as non-committal as possible.

A few more clicks of Ali's mouse, then, "Maggots."

"You know Ali," said Frank, irritation flushing his face with colour rather than a screen full of tomatoes that gave the glow to Ali's cheeks. "Both those examples are of species that doctors sometimes use to cure people. Leeches take away bad blood and maggots clear away dead flesh on otherwise healthy bodies. So, they're both really fucking useful to some poor sod of a patient, aren't they?"

Frank daren't look at Ali but kept his eyes firmly on his monitor. He took Ali's silence as a sign of sulking. He never meant to upset the kid, but sometimes he got right up Frank's nose. He double-clicked a bit too purposefully on a zipped file in order to expand it.

Frank was surprised when Ali muttered, "Sorry, Frank. I didn't mean that you were like that." Frank's anger, obvious in his voice, had clearly shaken the lad.

"I can't say that some paparazzi aren't 'like that' as you put it," Frank tried to explain in a more reasoned tone. "But honestly, Ali, I never met one."

"What about that lot that were bothering Gwyneth Paltrow outside that clinic when Chris Martin went for them?" asked Ali.

Frank had his own unfavourable opinion of Chris Martin, but, given Ali's passion for Coldplay's music, he wasn't about to share it.

"I think Chris Martin totally misread the situation. There was no threat to his wife whatsoever. Her mother was a celebrity before her, so Gwyneth's been around paps all her life and she's a pro at handling them. You may remember that on that occasion she just ignored the cameras, kept it buttoned, and got in the car. There was certainly no need for fisticuffs on Chris Martin's part, that's for sure."

He saw no point in telling Ali his opinion — that the reason Chris Martin often got upset at photographers was because he knew, in the early days anyway, they were only interested in his wife. Only about one person out of a hundred would have recognized the Coldplay band member whereas everybody knew Gwyneth Paltrow from her blockbuster films. A photographer couldn't give away a shot of Chris Martin, but a snap of the Hollywood star just walking down the street could pay thousands. Frank was convinced Martin had played the idiot just to get media attention. Frank didn't really like to talk about his days as a pap. For one thing he doubted if people who didn't know him back then would believe the stories, looking at what he'd become. But also, memories of those days filled him with sadness and anger at how much he'd lost. But in this instance, he felt compelled to try and explain to Ali.

"I'll tell you a story," he said, trying not to sound preachy. "A load of us were door-stepping outside the house where Kate Moss was having a birthday bash. Out comes Gwyneth and Chris and he goes apeshit because we're popping off shots of them. Talk about a dickhead! You've gone to Kate Moss's birthday bash — Kate Moss, mind you, the most sought-after model in Europe, not to mention all her A-list guests. Anybody with a brain in his head would realize the event was a paparazzo's wet dream. So how can you act all surprised and upset when you come out the front door with your film-star wife and a few flashes go off?"

"Maybe you were pushing them around or something," suggested Ali weakly.

"Honest, Ali — we were following them to the car, naturally — but nobody touched nobody. Anyway, I haven't finished. Another time, I was in Kauai following the Matt Leblanc wedding. All us paps were totally shut out, security tighter than a nun's nasty, and nobody could find a helicopter for love or money. If a celeb really wants to keep it private, they find a way. I'd spent a bloody fortune to get there. All flushed down the toilet, right?

"Totally by chance I bang into Gwyneth Paltrow, who's there on holiday. She recognized me and starts to give me a big speech about how she's on holiday and how she and her kids don't need me pestering them. I manage to get her attention long enough to explain that I wasn't there to follow her, that I'd come for the wedding but lost out. Then I suggest if we do some shots together, I'll promise on my mother's grave not to bother her for the rest of her holiday. She agrees and I take a bunch of photos made to look like they were grab shots. I sold them on and recouped my airfare and more. It saved my bacon and she got a peaceful holiday.

"The very next day after I did the shoot, I was at the airport and I bump into Chris Martin who comes across all chummy. He says that Gwyneth had told him the whole story, and he proceeds to buy me and the people I was with

Mojitos, or Mai Tais, or some other frigging concoction."

"Don't seem like the best situation though, does it?" said Ali. "To have to go to those lengths to get some peace and quiet on your holiday."

"Hardly lengths, was it, Ali? To take ten minutes or so to have me knock off a few good shots. And maybe she had a film coming out, or knew she looked good, all tanned and rested, so she figured it'd be a bit of positive publicity. I don't know, but I do know the situation isn't unusual. The photographer has his shots and the subject gets some good hype, it's a win-win situation."

Ali said nothing, his concentration seemingly focussed on his work. It never ceased to surprise Frank how the most vociferous critics were often silenced if the names of stars were invoked. It was as if his proximity to God-like celebs put people a little in awe of him, no matter how he'd ended up in their presence. He glanced across to try and read Ali's expression.

"What can you expect from a woman who names her daughter after a computer company?" asked Ali, smiling sheepishly at Frank.

"Very funny," said Frank, grinning with relief that Ali seemed persuaded. "But you do know, don't you Ali, that little Apple is probably named for the fruit?"

"Duh," said Ali, rolling his eyes.

Frank went back to downloading files and Ali closed the tomato photo on his screen and opened a similar close-up of a couple of peaches still attached to a leafy bough.

Frank thought about how careful he was to tread a fine line between trying to inform and guide Ali without appearing overbearing or pompous. At first, he'd been keen to be in Ali's good books solely to benefit from the wonder boy's knowledge of the digital world. But his consideration for Ali had grown into something less selfish. Frank supposed it must be the father in him. It was just a bloody shame he hadn't done as good a job with his own offspring.

"Paparazzi. Where does that word come from anyway?" asked Ali, hard at work restoring a brown spot on the skin of a peach to the same flawless light orange as the rest of its surface. "It sounds so gay. Paparazzi," he repeated it again giving it an over-the-top Italian emphasis.

Frank knew the term 'gay' had come to be used merely as a generally disparaging term, but it grated on his politically-correct 1970's sensibilities, especially coming from Ali.

"Paparazzo was the name of a character who was a photographer in a Fellini film back in the sixties," explained Frank. "Which was when the celebrity photo thing all started. It actually began in the 1940s and '50s, when photographs became easier to reproduce because of new printing methods. Newspapers and magazines began to pay humungous fees for pictures of criminals and film stars."

"Society being moulded by technology, as usual," muttered Ali.

Sometimes Frank was surprised by Ali's insights. God knows why he felt the need to father him, the boy was obviously as sharp as a tack.

"We could have had a worse nickname," said Frank. "They could have called us Secchiaroli after the real photographer who Fellini based his character on."

They were interrupted by the shrill electronic ring tone of Ali's extension.

"Ali speaking."

Frank heard the faint sound of a male voice on the other end of the phone.

"I'll come up," said Ali and rang off.

"The new boy in sales is having 'resolution issues,' whatever that means," said Ali. "And I'd pegged him for a fly one."

Frank remembered the fair-haired, blue-eyed Prince William look-alike who'd joined the agency the week before.

"Nice looking lad, though," said Frank.

"I hadn't noticed," claimed Ali. "I just hope he's not going to be having a lot of these 'blonde' moments, that's all."

"Careful, Ali," Frank called after the young Asian's retreating figure. "That comment is bordering on racism."

Frank worked diligently for fifteen minutes after Ali left. But his mind kept wandering back to his conversation with Donovan on the bus. He went over to Ali's computer and opened the Internet server. Frank scanned its History for the video of Kelly Anton. Once he discovered it, he clicked on it and waited for the song to start. As soon as the camera panned in, he paused the video. Frank gazed at Kelly Anton's face for a good thirty seconds. Then he closed the window and went into the menu to clear History. He clicked the Photoshop icon to return Ali's peaches to the screen. Frank walked over to where his jacket was hanging on a clothes hook behind the door of the windowless room. He fished Donovan's business card out of his pocket and stared for a second or two at the bright yellow paper and vivid purple ink. He closed the door and went back to his seat. After a minute of reflection, Frank reached for his phone, took a deep breath, punched a button for an outside line, and called the number on the business card.

"Welcome to Canary Records. How may I direct your call?"

"I'd like to speak to Donovan Carter, please," said Frank.

By mid-afternoon Kelly had dragged herself out of bed, away from Jason, who by then had his head in his iPad. She was enjoying the 'rain forest' shower head, as it was referred to in the flashy estate agent's brochure that had trumpeted the many luxurious features of the penthouse.

She was careful to keep her head out of the spray, but she lathered and rinsed the rest of her. It was one thing to let her hair resemble a rat's nest, but she was buggered if she was going to smell bad to match the dishevelled look Donovan wanted her to maintain — all part of his scheme to explain her so-called 'songwriter's block.' And there was only so much she could put over on Jason. He bought the story that her hair was her hairdresser's backcombed attempt at a 'retro' look, and he seemed to warm to his part in messing it up when they were in the clinches. But she knew he'd never countenance bad personal hygiene — she wouldn't want him to. So, she scrubbed away with gusto. Donovan never got close enough to know she smelt squeaky clean anyway. He'd never tried it on. Always the perfect gentleman in that respect, she'd give him that.

Kelly caught herself humming a few bars of a melody she'd dreamed up. She wished to hell she had words to go with it, something dark and disagreeable, because the notes were discordant, but in an interesting way. Kelly had first learnt how to read and write music from her father, who'd taught himself with a book and an old recorder someone had given him. By the time she started music lessons at school, she was way ahead of the other girls. The first time she heard the story of her father's youth, it hadn't made much of an impression. But as she grew older and began to better appreciate the hours he must have spent tooting on a worn recorder, struggling to differentiate between notes, the less she took his talents for granted.

She often thought about how, when she was small, she'd sit on his knee while he played the piano. She remembered the utter fascination she'd had with watching his hands stroke the keys. She was never more thrilled than when he occasionally shouted 'nah,' which was the signal for her to hit the keys he'd taught her, as he continued to play. As she grew, she graduated from his knee to a cushion on the piano stool beside him, eventually playing as many keys as him, in four-handed playing. Finally, he bowed to her superior skills and said "yuh doan be needin' mi no more,' and stood to watch her play. He'd sing along, often ad libbing, to whatever melody she came up with. Kelly hadn't realized until she was in her late teens what an extraordinary range her father had. She grew up believing every man could convincingly sing a female contralto, and then descend all the way down to the deepest bass, although she didn't know at the time what the different voices were called.

Her father's everyday speaking voice still carried a Jamaican lilt, and when he became overwrought, he lapsed into incomprehensible — to Kelly at least — patois. But in song he could mimic anyone's voice from the refined tones of Noel Coward, to the velvety cadences of crooner Johnny Mathis, to the East End exclamations of a British rapper. He only had to hear a style of singing voice once and he could imitate it. And not only the sound. He had the uncanny knack of being able to make up perfectly appropriate words for a song each voice might typically sing. When she was young, they'd played a game in which Kelly would play her father a few bars that she'd composed, and he had to not only mimic a voice to match but make up a few lines for a song the performer might sing. He almost never failed to do both, flawlessly. To great gusts of laughter from Kelly.

The only fly in the ointment was that he'd invariably stop the session by alluding to his failure in never having persuaded anybody to take a chance on his own voice and songs.

"Fuh why them record company men never take a flyer on me an' mi material?" he asked. His expression of hurt puzzlement was enough to make Kelly cry. Undeterred, her father continued writing songs for himself and the West

Indian band he jammed with, and with whom he sometimes performed at a couple of pubs and the occasional club. Kelly had once sat Donovan down and made him listen to a couple of the band's tracks, but he dismissed it as "ten-a-penny reggae." When Kelly first signed her recording contract, she wasn't sure how she'd break the news to her father, but he didn't show a single trace of resentment. He couldn't have beamed more broadly if he'd been the one to sign.

God, but she missed him — in more ways than one. She really must find a way to reconcile with him, it was the only way out of her present pickle. But each time she tried, they'd end up going hammer and tongs at each other about Jason. Her father didn't hold Jason responsible for any injustices his plantation-owner family may have been guilty of, that was past history as far as he was concerned. But he'd read — and believed — the lies that the tabloids had spouted about Jason. How could she make her father see that he wasn't the spoilt-rich-boy crackhead they made him out to be?

Her ruminations made Kelly think of the few lyrics she'd written for the evening's gig. She sang them, struggling to instil as much feeling as she could muster. She tried telling herself they weren't half bad, but deep down she knew they weren't up to the standard of her album tracks.

"Fuck, fuck, fuck," she said out loud, not knowing if it was herself, Donovan, or her father she was cursing.

Frank must have spoken to Donovan on the phone before, but he didn't remember that the nasal twang was exaggerated to the extent it was. Donovan sounded like a parody of himself.

"What can I do you for, Frank, my son?"

His son, for fuck's sake. If Donovan was actually his father, Frank would be serving a life sentence for patricide.

"I just happened to mention to my co-worker here that I bumped into my son-in-law, the record company executive, this morning," said Frank.

He knew Donovan would be flattered by the description.

"You didn't say nothing to your mate about Kelly's gig, did you, Frank?" asked Donovan.

"No, of course not. Mum's the word. But he asked me which company, and when I said Canary, he knew you had Kelly as an artist."

"Yeah, she's the jewel in the corporate crown, God 'elp us," said Donovan.

"Ali went on about what an amazing performer Kelly was ..."

He was beginning to lose his nerve. He worried that he sounded lame, to say the least. He told himself wouldn't have lost his bottle in the old days. Brazen bastard, he was. Best to get straight to the point.

"Anyway, Ali's really into hiphop, so I wondered if, as a great personal favour to me, you'd slip me a couple of tickets for the gig tonight for him and his girlfriend."

Frank doubted if Ali even had a girlfriend, or that he was into hip hop.

"I won't mention Kelly, I promise."

There was a brief pause. A muffled crackle on the line. Or it may have been Donovan clearing his throat, maybe chuckling. Although what the hell he'd have to laugh about Frank couldn't fathom. But then Donovan always was a weird little bastard.

"Glad to help, Frank. No worries, 'specially if it helps you in furthering your job prospects," said Donovan.

Frank winced, but he held it together.

"Thanks, Donovan. Really appreciate it."

"So, two passes at the door for ... what name is it?"

Passes. Shit. Frank should have guessed. He'd been to enough seedy clubs as an official photographer to know it wouldn't be tickets but a pass at the door for a specific person.

"You there, Frank?" the phone line crackled. "Whassis name?" asked Donovan.

"For Ali. Ali Khawaja."

"Come again?" said Donovan.

After Frank spelled it out, Donovan gave him the name and address of the club in Vauxhall — the Catacomb on the Albert Embankment.

"I hope for your Ali's sake as well as mine, Kelly keeps it together. But remember Frank, not a dickie bird to anyone, right?"

"On my honour," said Frank.

"Mmmm," murmured Donovan.

Frank said a fast goodbye, fearing he was about to lose it and ask what the hell Donovan meant by his doubting tone. After he put the phone down, he let out a long sigh.

"Wha's up Frank?" said Ali, as he walked back into the room.

"Nothing's up," said Frank. "Just in a bit of a quandary."

He had to think fast. Time was ticking, there were only a few hours left to get himself together. Which, Frank realized, was why he'd rung Donovan without really thinking things through. Making the pass in Ali's name had been a hasty mistake. Frank supposed he could claim his name was Ali Khawaja, but some bruiser of a bouncer was certain to clock Frank's Anglo-Saxon features and make waves. But he couldn't have told Donovan the pass was for himself. The canny bastard would have twigged immediately what Frank was up to. What was he up to, anyway? Was he really going to risk breaking the terms of his suspended sentence?

"Come on then, spill," said Ali. "I can't help you if you don't share."

He looked at Frank, eyebrows arched, lips pursed.

Frank hesitated. He knew he'd come to depend a hell of a lot on Ali's know-how, but could he trust him? Or maybe the bigger question was, should he even involve Ali?

Frank was well aware that he sometimes relied too much on his young co-worker. And not just for his computer expertise. Since Frank had sworn off alcohol, he'd made a point of eating healthier. Ali, being a vegetarian, had been a mine of information about things like leafy greens, beta-carotene-rich veggies, and high-fibre foods. Frank ate a lot of brown rice and beans, with carrots and kale. With his IT pay scale, Ali could afford the organic produce he swore by, but Frank's lowly salary wouldn't stretch that far. However, Frank could usually find the same non-organic items at his local Asda, and at his stage in life he doubted if a few chemicals would make much difference. Ali would have frowned at Frank's use of a microwave. He was convinced it sapped food of nutrients, but it was better than Frank's only other cooking appliance, an unreliable hotplate that came with his sparsely furnished bedsitter. Most nights after dinner Frank bundled up in bed to save on heating bills and thumbed through old computer magazines that Ali had given him. Ali was the only person with whom Frank had any meaningful conversation — apart from his AA sponsor, and the meetings of course, but they were always about the same thing.

Without thinking, he'd used Ali's name for the pass because he wanted the young geek's cooperation in this possibly insane — and possibly illegal — venture. But was it fair to get Ali mixed up in it? Would he be considered an accessory to Frank's breaking the conditions of his suspended sentence?

Frank continued to stare back at Ali, struck by the whites of the lad's eyes, pristine as poached eggs. Especially compared to Frank's own booze-blasted peepers with their network of blown-out blood vessels.

"Do you want to give birth so we can Christen?" said Ali.

He had many peculiar sayings, but Frank always found this one especially odd, coming from a Muslim.

"Okay," said Frank. "But keep an open mind."

"Don't I always?" asked Ali.

"You knew I was in trouble with the law, right?"

"There've been rumours. Never repeated by me, I hasten to add."

"Good, 'cos what I'm about to tell you goes no further than these four walls, right?" said Frank.

"I'd watch what you say around that Cheryl upstairs though, if I was you."

"Are you listening? Not a word to no-one."

"Scouts honour."

The fact that Frank knew full well Ali had never worn a Boy Scout uniform in his life — or that Ali was aware that Frank knew — didn't seem to matter. It was the earnestness in his voice that counted.

"A couple of years ago I was handed a suspended sentence for harassment and ABH ... Actual Bodily Harm, which is one step down from GBH, Grievous Bodily Harm."

"Does this hark back to our earlier conversation where you swore black and blue that paparazzi never bothered anyone, let alone laid a finger on them?"

"Very fucking funny," said Frank.

"Just trying to lighten the mood. You look as if you're about to burst a blood vessel. Take a load off," said Ali, pointing to Frank's computer chair. He sat down himself and wheeled his chair over to Frank's side.

"Whatever I said this morning, I'm not here to judge ... honest Frank. Just take a deep breath and tell me straight."

Christ, but the kid was insightful. He'd obviously seen something in Frank's expression to make him realize how much his opinion — approval? — meant. Frank sat and pulled his chair up to Ali's, so they were almost knee to knee. Frank glanced at the door, then leant forward.

"I was stitched up, I swear, Ali."

"I believe you. Thousands wouldn't," said Ali.

"I didn't even have my camera out — it was in my backpack with the rest of my gear — when this low-life second-rate musician nobody gives a toss about appears out of nowhere, starts yelling at me to leave him alone. Gets right in my face."

"So, you knew him?"

"Vaguely. He's a session musician. A saxophone player. I'd seen him at the odd gig. Always thought he was a bit mouthy. I'd heard him a few times boasting how he was Bruce Springsteen's go-to sax player when he was in Britain. Turns out he was once at a Springsteen concert in London 'cos he'd been hired to play with the warm-up band. The regular E Street Band saxophonist, Jake Clemens, nephew of the late, great Clarence, was taken sick just as the Boss and his mob were due to go on. They asked this wanker to step in for Jake. He did one solo riff and that was it, his sixty seconds of fame. But to hear him talk you'd think he was Springsteen's right-hand man."

"I presume a grab photo of him wouldn't be worth much?"

"Sweet fuck all. Who'd want it? He's a nobody. I couldn't even have told you his name back then."

"So, when he started up, you got physical?"

"Not at first. Well, okay, I may have pushed him off. He was right in my face, for Christ's sake. But it wasn't 'til he grabbed my bag and pulled out my camera that things got ugly. I went after my equipment, naturally. But before I could get hold of it, he threw the lot on the pavement, smashed the camera to smithereens. I totally lost it, of course. Beat the shit out of him."

"Wasn't there no-one around to witness what happened? That he'd provoked you?"

"That was the funny thing. All this went down right outside my old house, which was on a cul-de-sac in Notting Hill. Always quiet as the grave. And this was fairly early in the morning. I remember it like it was yesterday. I'd just come out the front door and was about to get in my motor to drop in on OK! magazine. I had an appointment with the new photo editor. There was nobody around when this obscure wanker first started in on me. But as soon as the fisticuffs began a couple turned up out of nowhere. Never seen them before. They both whipped out smart phones. I didn't know it at the time, but she was calling the police, and he was taking photographs of me beating the shit out of the saxophonist. Before I knew it, I was in handcuffs and the no-talent sax player was lying on the floor bleeding like a stuck pig."

Frank sat back and looked at Ali. Ali stared back at him his eyes slightly narrowed as if processing what he'd been told.

"And I suppose the mystery couple backed up his story that you were bothering him, and that your beating him was uncalled for?"

"Exactly. Then later, my darling son-in-law, who was supposed to be in court being a character witness for me, talked up this sax player like you wouldn't believe. To hear Donovan, you'd have thought this loser was a megastar whose name was on everyone's lips."

"Why would anyone listen to him?"

"Remember I asked you about Kelly Anton earlier? He's vice-president of her recording company."

Ali let out a low whistle.

"But you must have known other people who'd say his photo was worthless, and that there'd be no reason you'd ever want a shot of him?"

Frank looked down at his lap, he was gripping his thighs more tightly than he'd realized. He relaxed his hands and sighed.

"None of the editors were exactly supportive, they wouldn't stand up and say it. I was left with just a couple of other paps to back me up. And, believe it or not, Ali, paparazzi aren't exactly well thought of by people like judges and lawyers, who don't know fuck all about the business. I hired the one slightly bent barrister who took on paps as clients. He did his best, but the judge wasn't impressed. He made out he was being generous when he handed down a suspended sentence, said it was only 'cos it was a first offence that I wasn't off to jail. But he imposed a stipulation that I don't pick up a camera for five years, and not be within four hundred yards of any celebrity — whatever the fuck a celebrity is. And I had to attend anger management, blah, blah."

"Maybe you couldn't be a paparazzo no more, but you got to work with me," said Ali, grinning.

Frank managed a wry smile.

"That wasn't the end of it," he said. "It wasn't just the criminal case. The bastard took me to civil court. He claimed he couldn't play saxophone anymore 'cos one of his hands was mangled. Funny he hadn't mentioned it in the criminal case. I wouldn't have put it past him to hammer his own hand so he had x-rays of broken fingers. They awarded him massive costs. I was totally cleaned out. My wife divorced me and took what little I had left, and my daughter disowned me when I accused her husband of sabotaging my court case."

Frank let out the last few sentences in a torrent, as though, having started to fill Ali in, he couldn't stop. But he managed to come to an abrupt halt when he realized he was in danger of pouring out an account of his rage-fuelled binges after the court cases, ending up with a spell in hospital with alcohol poisoning. Even though he'd made it sound as if the court case was at the root of his divorce, and his estrangement from Whitney, it was actually the booze. If he hadn't been such an insufferable drunk, his daughter would have stood by him, no question. Ironic that the wake-up call for him to give up the demon drink came when he actually did wake up one day — in a hospital bed not knowing how he got there. He remembered staring, disbelieving, at the wraith-like appearance of the patient on death's door in the bed opposite. Frank knew at that moment that he'd soon be dead himself if he didn't clean up his act.

"That saxophone player must have been desperate for cash, to go to all that trouble," said Ali. "For all he knew you might have done a lot worse to him. What was the more serious one called? Grieving Bodily Harm?"

"Grievous," said Frank. "Even though he made a bundle from the civil case, I never really believed the reason he provoked me was to screw me for money. Like you said, he didn't have a clue how it'd all end up."

"What other reason could there be?"

"Fucked if I know," said Frank.

He'd often wondered if perhaps he'd had a run-in with the saxophone player when he was on a bender, and not remembered. There'd been more times than he could count when someone had come back at him for being an obnoxious bastard to them when he was drunk. Frank could never remember. He concluded after a while that he must be one hell of a nasty drunk. It hadn't stopped him from drinking again though.

"As difficult as that all must have been," said Ali. "Why are you crying to me about it now?"

"I need your help," said Frank.

"What a surprise. How? Doing what?"

"I want you to come with me ... well, actually it's the other way around. I'll be coming with you, since your name is on the passes."

"Where? What passes?" asked Ali. He was obviously

intrigued, not bothering to be his usual sardonic self.

"Again ... not a word, not a mention, not a whisper of this to anyone."

Ali rolled his eyes, but then nodded his head vigorously.

"Okay, okay," he said.

"To a surprise appearance of Kelly Anton tonight, in a small club in Vauxhall. With a bit of luck, you'll be mere feet from her."

Frank couldn't disguise his amusement when Ali's cool demeanour was completely shattered. The lad was clearly lost for words, his mouth hung open and he looked like he might piss himself with excitement at any moment.

"Trouble is we've got to figure out a way to pop off some shots without anybody knowing. Or more accurately, we've got to work out how you can pop off some shots, I not being allowed to pick up a camera."

The spell of the Kelly Anton name having dissipated slightly, Ali reverted to his usual style of banter.

"I know how to take a photo Frank. It's not brain surgery is it?"

"I don't doubt it for a moment Ali. Let's face it, with today's technology a five-year-old could take award-winning snaps. But what I haven't told you is that photography in this club is an absolute no-no. There's even a ban on mobile phones. According to my son-in-law, Kelly Anton doesn't want shitty pirate videos of her floating around on the internet."

"Why are we even talking about it then?"

"I remember you rabbiting on a couple of weeks ago about a friend of yours who was going to make a fortune out of a computer embedded in a pair of glasses."

"Yeah, Rashid. He's already got one of the big players interested. He's gonna be a fucking multi-millionaire."

"And if I recall correctly, you said these glasses had a camera?"

Ali emitted a low whistle. He'd obviously cottoned on to Frank's plan.

"You old fox, you," he said, eyes shining. "They do indeed. Rash managed the camera component really well. It can take eight-megapixel photos, which is better than it sounds, given he used a good-size sensor. The lens is excellent, and the whole thing has reasonable storage. Sixteen gigabyte flash memory. But it's slow, and the voice command might be glitchy. The micro-processor is just too micro."

Frank had no idea what Ali's techno speech meant.

"But if you were wearing Rashid's glasses, could you grab a few surreptitious photos? In a dark club?" he asked.

"Course," said Ali. "They just look like a pair of ordinary glasses, but with chunky frames."

"What about the light?"

"There's bound to be a good amount of light on the stage. And like I said, the sensor's a good size, which is what it's all about when considering light sources. A couple of the voice commands actually work okay. We'd probably be able to make those operate the camera so no-one would know I was taking photos."

"Can you transmit files right from the glasses?"

"Christ, Frank. Rashid may be clever but he's not Bill Gates — he doesn't have the whole of Microsoft at his fingertips. No, we'd have to download later using a USB cable before we send them anywhere."

No problem, thought Frank. Given there'd be no competition, no other paps peddling the same shots, there'd be no urgency in getting copies into photo editors' hands before anyone else. He smiled. God but it felt good to be back at it. He felt better than he'd felt for months.

"I don't know what you're grinning at," said Ali. "You may not be hefting a camera but given what you told me about your suspended sentence you'd be insane to go in there with me, given you said that Kelly Anton — a huge celebrity — will be mere feet away."

"I'm not letting you do this on your own."

"Are you afraid I'll cut you out of the deal?"

The words sounded fake, coming out of Ali's mouth. More like a line from a second-rate film he might have seen.

"Who said anything about a deal, Mr Big Shot?"

"Come off it, Frank. You obviously wouldn't be considering this unless there was a bundle to be made."

Frank needed Ali. He didn't have to think twice, and anyway, it was only fair that the kid would take part of the proceeds.

"You're right of course," said Frank. "So, here's the deal — you go in and take the shots, I'll peddle them to a couple of my old contacts, and we'll split the profit right down the middle."

"Really?" said Ali, his tough guy act had disappeared to be replaced by the wide-eyed naif Frank liked so much. "How much do you think you can sell them for?"

With the bait well taken, Frank decided not to mention Ali's past diatribes about the evils of paparazzi. He wasn't the keeper of Ali's conscience after all.

"Depends. Best case scenario is that she tanks, falls apart, obviously drunk or high — shots of that could make upwards of twenty grand, maybe more."

Ali's eyes opened even wider.

"Worst case: she comes on and does a good set with no problems, we'd probably only make five grand, if that."

"Let's hope she's out of her head then," said Ali.

Frank actually recoiled. His head jerked back, chin down, eyebrows raised. He was shocked at how quickly Ali — the rabid paparazzi hater — had turned around. Although why Frank was surprised, he didn't know. Experience should have told him that the prospect of a bunch of money in someone's hand can make the most solid of so-called principles drain away like water from a sink.

At first, Kelly felt miffed at the total lack of anybody who was remotely interested in her when she and Jason climbed out of the cab in front of the club in Vauxhall. If it had been one of her usual, well-advertised gigs, her handlers would have had to hustle her through the inevitable mob scene. Donovan had said she didn't need security staff, given nobody would guess she'd be at a little-known club hidden under a railway arch. But she hadn't believed him. She'd worn a headscarf and dark glasses, just in case. They were a waste of time. Not a single passer-by gave Kelly a second glance as she and Jason walked through the front door of the Catacomb.

When Kelly started to feel vaguely panicky that there was nobody bothering her, she realized she'd become too accustomed to pushy paps and ravening fans crushing the hell out of her. Was her fame so addictive that she felt the anxiety of withdrawal when it seemed to have been yanked away from her? Kelly asked herself if she was completely fucking mental. This was brilliant — like the good old days, when she could stroll into any venue with no hassle whatsoever. She supposed the guitar case that Jason had been kind enough to heft over for her might have pegged them as performers, but nobody seemed to give a toss.

Kelly had to admit Canary had been very generous when the company directors presented her with the Stratocaster after her album went diamond in America, back when they were still in their honeymoon period. Before that, in the days before she had a recording contract, Kelly had been her own roadie, dragging her acoustic guitar across London, lugging it up and down stairs of Tube stations and on and off buses. But since the album's phenomenal success, she'd become accustomed to sauntering into wherever she was performing carrying nothing except maybe a tea, leaving all the grunt work to somebody else.

It was good to have Jason along, and not just to carry her equipment. His calm presence almost made her forget her nervousness at not having much in the way of new material. The thought of it had been needling her, like the prospect of something painful, like a root canal.

The ease of arriving at the club helped Kelly's frame of mind, it prompted pleasant memories of what it was like — was it really only two years ago? — when she was just another musician, happy to have a gig. The tattooed girl on the door hardly looked up at them when Jason asked for the manager. Kelly supposed she wasn't expecting a recent superstar to be standing in front of her, so the penny hadn't dropped. As far as Kelly was aware only the manager had known she was coming, but even he, when he appeared, had a studied air of nonchalance, like the last thing he'd admit to was being impressed. Which was rare, usually even the most hard-bitten in the music business fell all over her. It occurred to Kelly he might have had his nose out of joint about the smart-phone ban.

"What a dump," whispered Jason in her ear as they trooped backstage behind the poe-faced manager. Kelly had been thinking how weird it was that she actually liked the grungy look of the place. All the walls had once been painted with black gloss. Since then, a slew of chips and scratches had been gouged out of the plaster, they stood out starkly, lurid white against greasy-looking surfaces. She doubted the place had been painted since '70s punks prowled the halls. Graffiti covered at least half the walls of the corridor they were walking down, some of it more legible than others, depending on the colour. Kelly was impressed by whoever had been inspired to use gold spray paint to write in massive capitals EAT THE RICH! She might normally be grossed out by the harsh sticky-floor noise her soles made on the cracked linoleum in the room they were shown in to — laughingly alluded to by the manager as her "dressing-room" — but the state of the floor just added to her appreciation of the alternative vibe of the place.

The only possible excuse for the dressing-room label was the presence of a clunky energy-saving light bulb dangling in front of a broken mirror mounted above a faux-marble Formica counter, spotted with ancient sticky rings of spilt liquid and a few scrunched-up tissues. Jason parked the guitar case and threw himself down on a sofa with a cover that might once have been pale green but was now so soiled any colour was difficult to identify.

Despite — or maybe because of — the cruddy atmosphere, Kelly felt a tingle of excitement. Sodding Donovan, he hadn't been far off the mark. If she did have a problem, this place might be just the jolt she needed. It reminded her of pubs and clubs she'd performed in when she started out. They might not have been quite so shabby, but something about the smell — hot dust and stale beer — thrust Kelly back to a time when she was as hyper with excitement as the flickering fluorescent lights in the corridor. She remembered how she used to quiver with positive energy before going on stage at places like the Catacomb.

Lately even the arena gigs weren't giving her what she needed — quite the opposite. They were too generic, too organized. Cars and drivers. Handlers. Choreographers, for fuck's sake. Posh dressing rooms, stuffed with every drink and snack imaginable, And, if whatever she fancied wasn't there, all she'd have to do is say the word.

More than once she'd asked a handler for the most outlandish thing she could imagine, just to see if she'd be given it. Jason knew about a rare black Japanese watermelon and, for a laugh, he told her to ask for it from the promoter at a tour stop in Manhattan. Sure enough, half an hour and a couple of thousand dollars later, the melon appeared, on ice and ready sliced. If it hadn't been for the millions the promoter must have been making out of Kelly's act, she might have felt guilty. Especially since it didn't taste much different from a green watermelon that only cost a quid down in Battersea market.

Sure, the roar from several thousand throats was amazing, and the terror of standing in front of a massive crowd could be motivating, to say the least. But now she realized she'd missed the intimacy of smaller venues. She was remembering, with excited anticipation, how she was able to see the looks of awe on punters' faces in places like the Catacomb, even those at the back of the room, when she nailed it.

From the stage at the end of the corridor Kelly could hear the repetitive phrasing of a rapper, or was it hip-hop? Maybe grime? She'd been deep into all that stuff once. Watched Channel U along with her mates and been as handy as the next kid with names for every genre and sub-genre. She knew the more political element claimed not to care about sales and money, they just wanted to get the message out — against poshification, racism, globalization, the police. No doubt she was dissed for making bucket-loads of cash, maybe by the tossers who were on stage right then. She got that, for them, it was all about the words, but to her, words meant fuck all if there was no melody or interesting cadence. She'd been royally pissed off when Tinie Tempah knocked her off the top spot with his boring-as-shit debut single. She had to concede the lyrics were brilliant, but musically you'd get more out of a didgeridoo.

"Wotcha!"

Donovan's head appeared round the door before he sidled into the room. He was wearing one of his shiny flash Italian suits and grinning like an idiot. Kelly thought he looked like a fox that's caught the cat that drank the sodding cream. He was carrying one of those moulded cardboard trays that held two disposable coffee cups.

"Not sure about this venue, Donovan," said Jason from his perch on the couch. "If the kids who're likely to come here put their pennies together they still wouldn't have enough to buy a single, let alone a whole album."

"I hadn't realized Little Lord Fauntleroy here was your manager now, Kelly," said Donovan. "And after I've gone and bought a latté for you both, and all. Ungrateful bastard."

"You know I don't drink coffee, Donovan." Kelly couldn't count the number of times she'd told him. He never remembered.

"Pass it over, I'll have one," said Jason.

"I should bloody throw it over, not pass it over," said Donovan, but he handed the tray to Jason.

"Anyway, Jason's not far wrong, is he?" said Kelly. "This place is a rat's nest, and I don't only mean metaphorically."

She was buggered if she'd give Donovan the satisfaction of knowing she liked the place.

"What do you care if it's not the Ritz?" asked Donovan. "I'm not asking you to move in. All you have to do is do your thing on stage and sod off."

The sound of applause and heartfelt whoops echoed down the hall. It sounded like the first act had crashed to the close of their first set.

"What you even here for, anyway?" asked Kelly. "I didn't know you was gracing us with your presence."

"Just wanted to make sure you performed like we agreed," said Donovan.

"What you goin' to do if I don't? Drag me off the frigging stage."

Voices in the corridor had grown louder, then petered out. Kelly assumed it had been the hip-hoppers, rappers, or whatever they were, heading for another room down the hall.

"Come on then, the assistant manager is going to announce a 'special appearance' for the break — that's you, Superstar."

"Don't I need to do a line first, or shoot up, or whatever?" asked Kelly, in an innocent little-girl voice — her attempt at sarcasm.

"Very fuckin' funny," said Donovan.

"Break a leg, darling," said Jason. He stood up to kiss her on the cheek, then settled deeper onto the dirty couch.

Christ, thought Kelly. In the heat of her exchange with Donovan she'd forgotten Jason. He might be wondering what she was on about, being a smart-ass about taking drugs, which he knew she never did. She still hadn't had the nerve to fill him in on her and Donovan's subterfuge. All he knew was that Donovan was giving her time to come up with new material. But the more the press portrayed her as drug-addled, the guiltier she felt, because more and more often they were smearing Jason too.

"Bye babe, see you in a bit," she said breezily, as she grabbed her guitar and followed Donovan out of the dressing-room door. As she left, she saw Jason throw aside his empty coffee cup and pull out the small wooden container that he called his 'crack-in-a-box.' He once told Kelly the box had come with half-a-dozen cigars, a gift to his father from a Cuban diplomat. Jason was taking a chance bringing paraphernalia to the club, but Kelly supposed it'd relieve his boredom. She'd told him he didn't need to catch her on stage, that it was bound to be mental inside the club. Jason had looked slightly hurt but agreed maybe it was for the best. Kelly was relieved on two fronts — she wasn't sure about the new stuff, and if she went along with what Donovan wanted her to do, she didn't want Jason seeing. Better he stayed in the dressing room, even if he was a little blitzed. But Kelly had never known Jason to be totally off his face, he was always careful. He often went days without anything stronger than an occasional beer. Nevertheless, she worried about him.

But as soon as she was out in the dingy hall, all thoughts of Jason fled. She felt a not-unpleasant gut flutter. She relished a bracing, nervy face-tingling that she hadn't experienced for years. So much more positive than the total terror before the last few mega-concerts. As her performance jitters had increased, Donovan was at her to try all kinds of strategies to overcome it. Books he made her read about stage fright with all their advice about 'employing the fear in the work' were lost on her. Alcohol — a single barley wine — did the trick to a certain extent, but she was fucked if she was going any further down that road and end up another member of the '27 club.' Janis Joplin, Brian Jones, Jimi Hendrix, Jim Morrison, Kurt Cobain — all dead at twenty-seven-years-old. On Donovan's insistence, she'd been to see a therapist, an ex-classical trumpet player, who'd been forced to retire due to crippling performance anxiety. He was reputed to work wonders, but they'd got off on the wrong foot when she asked him how come, if he was so clever at fixing stage fright, he wasn't back tooting his horn in the Albert Hall? She knew she was being a bitch, but she also knew the root of her problem was the ever-present spectre of the new material she didn't have. Until that was sorted, she was well and truly screwed — and she didn't have a clue how to fix the situation.

"You haven't forgot what we agreed, have you Kelly?" said Donovan as they neared the opening to the stage, a rectangle of blinding light. "One of your classic hits to remind the bastards whose amazing presence they're in. Followed by the new number in your impeccable style. But then it's time to crash during the last oldie but goldie, right?"

"Mmm." Kelly's distracted muttering belied the zing she was feeling. It reminded her of when you're just on the edge of doing something super-scary but that could also be super-fun, like going down the bullet water slide at East Park, where her Mum sometimes took her. She felt her whole body vibrating with nervous energy.

"You listening?" said Donovan.

"Yeah, yeah. Don't get your knickers in a knot."

A handsome kid wearing a peaked cap too big for his head, and trousers with the arse down at his knees, appeared out of the shadows. He was holding a wireless microphone.

"This is Kayden. He's going to introduce you and handle the sound," said Donovan.

"Kelly ... really pumped to meet you. Huge fan."

"Pleasure's mine, darlin'" said Kelly.

The kid grinned like he'd won the lottery. Kelly had come to know when people in the business were brown-nosing — it happened more often than not. This kid's complete and obvious lack of ass-kissing attitude was as refreshing as a cool drink on a hellishly hot day.

"So, you'll prompt sound when I give you the signal, right?" said Kelly as gently as she could.

"Yeah, for sure. Donovan gave me the play list."

"All right then," said Kelly.

Kayden gave her another dazzling smile and bounded on stage. He immediately started his patter, but Kelly didn't take it in. She was taking deep lung-filling breaths in an attempt to control her heart, which was in danger of jumping out of her chest. She was only jolted into action by Kayden shouting her name and the few astonished whoops that followed.

"... here she is, Kelly Anton herself."

Once inside the Catacomb, Frank made a mental note to remember to wipe his feet on the way out of the place — he doubted if the floor had been cleaned since the millennium.

He hadn't been able to resist tagging along, despite being painfully aware of Ali's earlier observation that he'd be in the shit if anybody saw him within shouting distance of Kelly Anton, a 'celebrity' like the ones he'd been ordered to stay away from. He'd told himself that as long as he kept his head down, he'd be fine. Trouble was, being such an obvious square peg in a very round hole was cranking up Frank's paranoia.

Before the girl on the door — more inked and pierced than a tattooist's wire-bound catalogue — had looked up Ali's name and let them in she'd given Frank a bemused once-over, as if to say 'what the fuck are you doing here.' Once inside, Frank felt about as old as an Egyptian mummy — not one other person appeared to be much more than eighteen-years-old, although a few of the boys were scarily cocksure, given their tender years. And Frank couldn't help thinking that every kid in the club, if asked, was likely to remember the old guy lurking at the back of the room, like a paedophile at a playground. Frank prayed they'd assume he was a bouncer and think no more about it. He reckoned he looked only slightly older than the one who was certainly taking his job seriously, inspecting bags and frisking everyone at the entrance.

"If he was any more thorough, he'd have to marry me, innit," Ali muttered after he'd been patted down and shoved aside.

Frank tried to adopt the assertive yet bored expression that he'd seen on bouncers' faces in every club he'd ever been kicked out of. He'd told Ali — and himself — he'd better be there in case Ali needed help, but the lad had adopted the paparazzo persona like he'd been at it for years. Frank could see he'd managed to work his way up front, so he had an unobstructed view of the stage through his mate, Rashid's, magic goggles.

Frank had been surprised when Rashid turned out to be tall and fit, looking more Bollywood heartthrob than computer geek. Before the gig the two lads had spent a half-hour in a quiet corner of a pub in Pimlico, chosen as their HQ for the evening because of its proximity across Vauxhall Bridge to the Catacomb, fixing up the miraculous spectacles to be able to voice-activate the camera release. Frank thought they'd pee their pants when, after a couple of false starts, Ali managed to capture and download a pin-sharp shot of Rashid, who'd been standing at the bar a good thirty feet away.

"What's the magic phrase that triggers the shutter?" asked Frank.

Ali had said something that sounded like it came from an Indian restaurant menu, "something paneer."

"What's it mean?"

"It's Urdu for 'Say cheese!'" said Ali, which had sent the two lads into paroxysms of giggles.

If Frank were honest, he'd have to admit that the real reason he'd gone to the Catacomb was because he was ultra-curious to see Kelly Anton in the flesh. Not because of her fame — he actually felt relieved, once the shock of losing his livelihood lessened, not to be chasing glitterati 24/7. Contrary to people's assumptions about the celebrity/paparazzo dynamic, Frank had been used and abused by enough so-called superstars to last several lifetimes. It was just that the video of Kelly had been playing in his brain like an audio-visual ear worm. He couldn't believe a live performance could be as brilliant — there had to be some post-production enhancement of image and sound. Nobody was that blinding in real life. He had to see, and hear, for himself.

But first he was subjected to the lad who was on stage doing whatever it was he was doing — 'chanting' was the only way Frank would have described it. His deep voice and references to 'knives,' 'guns,' and 'gaping pussy' didn't match his slight physique and elfin face, more mischievous than murderous. But the rapturous crowd didn't seem to care, they bobbed furiously to the constant and unwavering backbeat, arms up-stretched, fingers either pointing to heaven or straight at the stage. Frank had to admit the backing — whirling electronica, odd voices, undistinguishable urban noises — added an intriguing contrast to the monotony of the vocals. Whether he couldn't take seriously the violent ghetto talk coming out of this unprepossessing young man's mouth, or he was grooving on the not-unpleasant hypnotic quality of the overall sound, he wasn't sure, but he found himself enjoying it.

Between numbers a chubby lad standing next to Frank, with only the slight suggestion of hair on his top lip, said, "I's mad innit?"

"Yeah, it's ... really good," Frank said, hoping to hell that's what the kid meant.

"It straight street, he never polish nothing on that. It turn them others into a bat boy, i's mad."

Frank translated the kid's obviously heartfelt statement as meaning the lyrics were raw and without compromise, making more commercial performers seem insincere.

"Brave," was all Frank could think to say. But what went through his head was: How is it possible to feel that you inhabit a completely different galaxy — let alone another planet — from a room-full of fellow Londoners?

"He done two year for gun possession," said the kid, as though it were some kind of qualification, the equivalent of an M.B.A. for an aspiring executive.

After the next number, which turned out to be the last of the set, the kid turned to Frank.

"You caan' even control what them words do to you, once they gets in you." He thumped his chest, and stared at Frank, tongue-tied and misty-eyed.

Obviously, the messages in the words, many of which Frank couldn't decode because of the street slang, touched the lad somewhere deep. The boy's tears evoked a wave of empathy in Frank. He'd been wrong to dismiss the lyrics — if they could be described as such — as melodramatic bravado. They were clearly more genuine than most. Not to Frank though, he hadn't had the necessary experience, but to the lad, and doubtless to every young person in the place, who waved and pointed throughout in an intense display of solidarity, the words touched a massive nerve.

Back in the day, Frank had leant towards the more shit-disturbing musicians, The Who, The Animals, the Stones, when they weren't being narcissistic, sometimes Bob Dylan, but he'd never felt as keenly about a song as this boy obviously did. The thought occurred to Frank that the groups he'd listened to hadn't had as urgent an agenda as the performer he'd just heard, they certainly weren't as invested in an outcome, if there was to be any.

His thoughts were interrupted by a guy on stage announcing a "massive musical talent …."

The crowd weren't paying much attention. Some just stood around, appearing stunned by the act they'd just seen. Some were clearly pumped, talking excitedly over each other and waving their hands in each other's faces. Some were making for the bar at the back of the room, looking like they might drop if they didn't have sustenance.

"… here she is, Kelly Anton herself."

Frank strained to see the stage. He heard someone say, "'e's 'aving a laugh, innit."

69

But heads dodged around for a better view. The talkers were silenced. Even people heading for the bar stopped in their tracks and turned. The tall young man on stage looked toward the side, one arm outstretched in a welcoming manner.

Frank had seen some wild audiences in his time but when Kelly walked on stage and began strumming a few chords to test sound, he couldn't believe such a wisp of a woman could create such a shit storm of a reaction. The room went berserk. Not just the noise — whistles, whoops, some people bellowing "Kelly" like they'd spied a long-lost friend on the other side of the street — but the rush to get nearer to her, which happened so quickly that if Frank had blinked, he'd have missed it. In just a few seconds, a crowd that had filled the whole space from front to back was crammed into only the front two-thirds of the club. Frank hoped Ali wasn't having the life crushed out of him against the stage.

No matter how many times Frank had witnessed the peculiar — and obviously irresistible — urge of people to be near a so-called star, he'd never understood it. It was one thing to be one of the hormonal teenagers screaming hysterically at Paul McCartney or Mick Jagger that he'd seen back in the day, but Frank had since witnessed perfectly sane, sophisticated adults push others to the ground to reach the side of a 'celebrity.' And then what? Touch the hem of their garment? Mumble some inanity, like 'love your work?' Most people just grinned idiotically, completely tongue-tied, until a security goon moved them along.

He was surprised that this crowd, who in their way had displayed as much agitprop as any leftie activist he'd ever encountered in their reaction to the mention of privilege from the previous act, were so gaga about Kelly Anton. They had to be aware she was a multi-millionaire. Maybe that was why. She'd bucked the system, succeeded, despite whatever disadvantage she might have had in common with these kids. Frank remembered the effect her video had had on him and decided maybe it was little wonder they couldn't get close enough.

Frank had a perfectly good view of the stage from his position at the back of the room. He watched as Kelly stood gazing out at the crowd, unsmiling, face immobile. He had the feeling she wasn't necessarily basking in the adoration. With her chin slightly raised, it seemed to Frank almost as if she were saying "Bring it on!" Challenging the audience, but to what? The longer and louder the cacophony continued the more she appeared to grow in stature, but it seemed to him as if she were gathering forces for a fight rather than collecting herself for a performance. The crowd seemed to thrive on her fierce-as-fuck look and yelled all the more. Eventually she looked to the side. As the opening bars of music threatened to drown out the audience, Kelly looked down at her feet, obviously waiting for her cue. The crowd roared all the louder, as if battling the sound of the music. But as soon as Kelly looked up and started to sing, the noise fell away, like a classroom of noisy kids quieted by a single look from a ferocious teacher.

IT TOOK A minute or so for the room to go wild — not until she'd strummed a few chords for sweetheart Kayden to adjust sound. At first there'd clearly been mass scepticism. Kelly could almost hear the mutters, "Yeah right, Kelly Anton, my arse." But, when the realization hit the crowd that it was actually her, the real deal, standing live in front of them, even the coolest club-goer couldn't hold back. She knew half the kids in the room probably didn't rate her, some might actively dislike her stuff. But she'd learnt never to underestimate the power of celebrity.

Since the platinum and diamond albums, the millions of YouTube hits, and — even more so — all the tabloid and MTV crap about her and Jason's so-called dope-fuelled goings-on, there wasn't a single music fan, no matter how jaded, who didn't get wet knickers or a hard-on in her presence. The tumult of feverish adulation in the low-ceilinged club was as reassuring as her mother's hugs. The fight-or-flight adrenalin gave up on goading her to run for the hills and switched her to confrontation mode. Her heart slowed, the palms of her hands dried. Despite bright stage lights, she could see the whole room beyond. She stared out, face motionless, taking in every detail of the frantic crowd.

There was a guy at the front who caught her attention. He was the only one not whooping or clapping. He wore glasses with dark frames that reminded her of Jarvis Cocker's, but this kid's were even heavier. He barely moved. Just stared, like he was catatonic, yet his lips moved, as if he were talking to himself. Kelly assumed he was in shock at seeing Kelly Anton more or less within touching distance. Shit, what a rush! She should do all her concerts as surprise events.

Kayden was now off to the side, ready to cue the recorded sound for her first number. She turned her head and gave him a nod. The opening bars of 'It's Like I'm Outside' boomed across the room. At first the crowd's cacophony doubled with recognition of the song. Then, as she began the first line, they quieted. The hush of appreciation gave Kelly as much of a rush as the cheers.

"The night draws down
Rude girl out on the town
Living it large in the bar
It's like she's outside
Just watching the ride"

Kelly had once flirted with Kundalini yoga after she heard it would release female energy coiled at the base of her spine. But she sprained her neck doing one of the poses and could never stop thinking about music or Jason's body long enough to empty her mind and meditate, so she gave it up as a lost cause. But now, with each line sung, she felt as if that mythical Kundalini cobra were rising up her spine. Energy radiated throughout her entire body, reaching as far as her toes and her fingertips. Every part of her — particularly her throat and lungs — felt lubricated, like a proverbial well-oiled machine. As she sang the last chorus, she felt the ecstasy of absolute control.

She was so in-the-moment she didn't think about the times when she'd been so shit-scared that she'd fallen apart. She was, however, aware of the amazing exuberance that comes with the removal of some massively inert blockage. There was no high like it as far as Kelly was concerned. Nothing even came close — not even sex. The audience noise was minimal, a few singing along, but all faces were zeroed in on her, like a vast field of sunflowers following the sun. A sea of upraised arms, waving euphorically, let her know there wasn't one person who wasn't fully engaged, right there with her. She was enjoying herself so much when the song approached the end that she sang the last verse all over again. Without recorded accompaniment she did it with only her guitar, which allowed her to throw in a few change ups here and there for the hell of it.

"She's fake and she's snide
But she can't turn the tide
And now she can't love her
Herself nor no other
Just a girl in a bar
Struggling not to be smother
And it's like she's outside
Just watching the ride"

She wasn't surprised when her new song didn't go over quite so well, nevertheless she was totally thrown by the reaction. The crowd was respectful, but there was a lot less arm waving and definitely no blissful expressions. She tried telling herself it was because it was unfamiliar to them, or because the only accompaniment was her guitar, but deep down she knew the words didn't hold any depth of feeling. She knew the spilling-of-guts element in the lyrics — that had leant magic to the album tracks — simply wasn't there. She was certain the melody was as amazing as any she'd written, so she tried a bit of scat instead of words. But some "da-dee-da" and "pip-pippa-pipee" was way too jazz-club for this crowd — it would have been even for her regular audience come to that. And she wasn't accustomed to doing it. Ella Fitzgerald might have nailed it, but not Kelly Anton. There was a smattering of applause, but people were already shouting out titles of her previous hits before she sang the last note of the new song. Kelly was aware that the sudden halt in the flow of whatever chemical her brain produced when she was on top of things was probably as bad or worse as withdrawal from any man-made drug. She could feel a stomach-churning plunge of energy, a quivering of her legs.

She looked over at Kayden to prompt the next song, one of her old ones. He must have sensed her panic, because his million-volt grin had been replaced by a furrowed forehead and narrowed eyes. She tried a smile, but knew it didn't look right, she was somehow unable to find the right facial muscles. All she could think about was that she'd never have a good song ever again. The crushing loss she felt was the most debilitating she could ever remember feeling. She watched desolately as Kayden flicked a switch. The opening bars of another track from the album boomed out.

The crowd had the same tumultuous reaction as before,

but this time it wasn't the quality of her voice that quieted them. She came in a beat or two too late. It was her hesitation, and the total lack of sync with the instrumental as she stumbled over words, that prompted a stunned hush from the crowd. Any memory of lyrics was wiped out by the utter desolation she was experiencing. She stopped and stood, silent, staring at her feet as the music continued. She roused herself and tried to come in on the fifth line. She managed to hold it for the rest of the verse, but she knew her voice was as weak and off-key as a drunk at karaoke night down the pub. All she could think was "what if" … "what if all the songs she penned were rubbish." She came up empty for the beginning of the next verse, couldn't remember a word. But the recorded melody wore relentlessly on. There were a few boos and a jeer or two.

Kelly was aware that adoration could melt away as fast as morning frost on a sunny pavement, but she was stunned at how quickly the room had turned. She stared at the guy at the front who was still gazing back at her through his thick-framed glasses. There seemed something scarily freaky in the way his lips continued to move. She was glad the stage lights reflected off his lenses — she was weirded out enough without seeing his eyes. She managed to start the next verse on time, but her voice was no stronger and she completely ran out of steam — and breath — before the chorus. Fear-induced adrenalin swamped her. The flight compulsion overwhelmed her. It gave her just enough energy to flee the stage.

W<small>HEN KELLY LAUNCHED</small> into her first song, that amazing voice resonating throughout the room, Frank's scalp tightened to such a degree that the sensation was downright unpleasant. Rather than being less than her recording,

Kelly was so much more impressive, belting it out in front of an audience. Frank whooped and clapped with the rest of the room after she finished the amazing unaccompanied final verse. Frank realized he was blinking back tears. Christ! he thought, I'm almost as emotional as the chubby kid had been earlier. He thought about when he heard the song for the first time earlier in the day, and how moved he'd been. The words described his own experience so perfectly. 'Feeling fake, unable to turn the tide, struggling not to be smothered, like being outside himself.' Frank grimaced to think that he now understood better why the lad had been so affected. When anybody hears their own story, it's certain to blow their mind.

Only a couple of minutes into Kelly's second song — introduced briefly as "something new" — Frank could sense the change in the atmosphere, as noticeable as a swift drop in temperature. As the energy slowly seeped out of the club, Kelly's voice became less powerful and more tentative. One by one, people gave up on swaying and pointing. The crowd appeared restless. At the end of a respectful smattering of applause, it seemed to Frank that Kelly shrank. Her cocky, almost scornful, demeanour had morphed to hesitant glances at the crowd in front of her.

The sound of the next song's music, clearly familiar to the crowd, energized the room somewhat, but the renewed energy quickly fled when it became obvious Kelly was having trouble. She stopped after a couple of lines and stared at her feet. Frank was willing her to continue. She did, but weakly, stumbling over words. After totally losing her way, Kelly looked around distractedly. She focussed her gaze off to the side from where she'd come and headed off in that direction, disappearing from view. Almost immediately the kid who'd introduced her ran on to the stage.

"The legendary Kelly Anton, people," he intoned, as if nothing untoward had happened. But his expression showed he was as confused as the audience. Some people booed, a couple of people shouted out that Kelly was "out of 'er tree," and other expressions to that effect. The kid did his best to offset an obvious atmosphere of disappointment. "In five minutes, Giggs, back for a second explosive set," he announced. Frank thought, not for the first time, how quickly the tide can turn. Adulation had transformed to puzzlement, and then to downright disdain, accompanied by shaking of heads and muttering, all in the space of mere minutes.

Frank felt himself becoming angry at the crowd on Kelly's behalf. Fickle fuckers, in his opinion. He glared at a few of those closest to him. But then he wondered why he was upset. He'd seen enough displays of negative reaction to a performer without it getting to him, and it wasn't as if Kelly deserved better necessarily. She had, after all, crashed spectacularly. He took a few deep anger-management breaths and told himself he must be getting soft in his old age. If he'd been this way when his livelihood depending on it, he'd never have lasted ten minutes.

At that moment Ali appeared, pushing his way through the melée. He seemed distinctly uneasy. His normally healthy colour had taken on a green tinge.

"Let's get out of here before that naff rapper comes back," he said. "I want to get back ASAP. I'm shit scared we might have nothing."

"What the hell makes you think that?" asked Frank.

"I was sure Rash incorporated the camera release noise. There isn't a shutter as such, but most devices duplicate the noise to let users know they've taken a picture. I couldn't hear it at all."

Frank was surprised to find he didn't care, almost hoped the magic glasses had fucked up. He'd be happy if there was no record of Kelly's fifteen-minute plummet from goddess to has-been. He was sorry to leave. He'd have loved to catch more of the rapper, if that's what he was. And to see the effect he had on the crowd. But Ali was already hustling them out.

"I tell you what though, Frank. If I did get shots, there's going to be some corkers when she crashed and burned. I was on the side of the stage where she did her disappearing act, so I could see her clear as day. Out of her head."

Frank wasn't convinced Kelly was as 'out of her head' as Ali thought. She hadn't stumbled, or staggered, or anything else that trashed people did, drunk or high. She'd scurried purposefully off stage. As they headed back to the pub where Rashid would be waiting to download whatever images the miraculous glasses had captured, Frank thought about Kelly's appearance. He'd seen enough lushes and druggies to know when someone was intoxicated. He didn't think Kelly had any of the droopy-eyed, unfocussed look dopeheads display. And how could she have gone from being so completely in control for the first number to totally at sea in less than a couple of minutes. Unless she'd popped something while on stage, but he didn't think so. No, if anything her face had been ultra-alert, more like someone terrified than inebriated. But if he was right, why had Donovan been so insistent Kelly was a drug-addled mess?

As they walked over the bridge, the river swirling below them, the tide obviously on the turn, Frank glanced over to his other side, at Ali. The lad's brow was furrowed. He stared intently ahead as if willing them to arrive at their destination — the pub, and Rashid — faster. Frank knew he was desperate to download whatever shots he'd managed to grab. He knew only too well the anxiety Ali must be feeling. Frank had experienced it every day of his professional life — the worry, bordering on panic, before a photo was actually in the bag and delivered, out of his hands. Frank was pleased to discover he felt none of the jitters he used to experience. He supposed that Ali's photos, some of them — the most saleable — would show distress etched into Kelly's face as she stumbled off the stage. He thought about being pissed off at the crowd for turning so swiftly from adoration of her to undisguised scorn. Were he and Ali any better for wanting to make money out of the situation? At that moment Frank realized he couldn't care if the shots worked out or not, despite the trouble he and Ali had gone to.

"TALK ABOUT ACADEMY Award winning performance," Kelly heard Donovan say as he trotted along behind her up the clammy corridor, backstage of the club. "Bleedin' Meryl Streep couldn't have done better."

Kelly increased her pace. She didn't want Donovan to clue in to the fact that there'd been no acting the drugged-out rock star on her part. She may not have been off her head, but she'd been genuinely freaked — like all the times before — by the idea of never again having any good lyrics. The horror of it had totally robbed her of the ability to sing one of the hits she'd performed so often she should have been able to belt it out, no matter what. All she wanted at that moment was to get inside the excuse for a dressing room as fast as she could and close the door on Donovan, not to mention the rest of the world. She craved the safe haven of the all-enveloping arms of her man, she couldn't give a shit if that made her girlie, more Mills & Boon than Cosmo.

Having recognized the door by the scrawl of fluorescent orange spray-paint — CLAPTON IS GOD — Kelly threw it open, intending to turn on Donovan immediately and tell him to piss off. But her eye caught sight of Jason sprawled awkwardly, his legs akimbo on the filthy sofa, his torso and head dangling just above the floor. One arm was flung out to the side, the other lay across his chest. Given his awkward position it was clear to Kelly something was seriously wrong.

"Jason! For fuck's sake."

She heaved him up onto the sofa and grasped his face on either side of his mouth. She shook his head. His eyelids opened briefly, but all she could see was mostly the whites as his eyes rolled back in his head.

"Jason! Jason babe!"

She slapped him a couple of times, hardly noticing Donovan looming over her.

"At least the silly bastard's still breathing ... barely," he said.

"Don't just stand there making stupid remarks, call a fucking ambulance," yelled Kelly.

Donovan moved away. Kelly continued to slap and shake Jason, willing him into consciousness. She could hear Donovan speak to the operator as casually as if he were chatting with a mate.

"Drug overdose. Probably crack, that's his usual tipple, if you can call it that."

If Kelly hadn't been so intent on trying to wake Jason, she swore she'd have throttled Donovan.

"Catacomb. It's a club on Albert Embankment in Vauxhall," he continued. "Quick as you can. He don't look too bright, if you catch my drift."

"Matter of minutes, apparently," he said, once he'd disconnected, as cool as if he was announcing a taxi's arrival time.

"Well, get out front and find them," screamed Kelly. "They won't know where the fuck we are in here, will they?"

Once Donovan had left, Kelly realized that Jason's 'crack-in-a-box' was sitting on the couch, next to him.

The box appeared to be tightly closed, so nobody would see the contents — the couple of cling-film twists of crack, Jason's glass pipe, and the old zippo lighter he liked to use — but she thought she'd better stash it somewhere. Christ knows why, Donovan had already announced crack was involved when he spoke to the emergency operator. She supposed she was hoping against hope that Jason's overdose, if that's what it was, could be kept under wraps. She knew she ought to be freaking about Jason's survival — and she was — but also the last thing she needed was for her father to get wind of the episode. She grabbed the box and stuffed it into a pocket of her coat, which was draped over the back of the couch where she'd left it. It seemed like hours 'til the emergency-response bods arrived, but Donovan, who seemed to have timed it like a nerdish schoolboy, insisted it was only seven minutes from when he'd phoned.

Kelly had to admit, once the two uniformed paramedics burst into the dressing room, they moved at lightning pace. First thing they did was demand of Kelly what Jason was on. Once she'd confirmed it was crack, one of them, a slight woman wearing more make-up than Kelly would have expected — Tracey, according to her name tag — had Jason on oxygen and hooked up to a drip in mere seconds. She attached a clothes-peg thingy to Jason's finger, with a meter device on the other end that beeped when she poked it. The other paramedic, a bulky guy with an astonishingly large bum, injected something into Jason's arm.

"What's that then?" asked Kelly, trying to appear calm and coherent.

"Valium," said the big-assed man.

Kelly glanced at the name on his badge, pinned to his chest: Trevor Williams.

"They often get a bit frisky when they first come round. This mellows them out," he said.

"*If* they come round," said Donovan, interrupting a phone call he was making.

"You're a big help," said Kelly. "And who the fuck are you on the blower to, at a time like this."

"He's breathing well, and his vitals aren't too bad," said the woman.

"Still, we need to get him to A&E lickety spit, just in case," said Trevor Williams.

Having stressed the need for speed it seemed to Kelly they took aeons to get Jason onto the gurney. Then they took a while to hook up the drip to the gurney. Kelly was slightly reassured when she saw that Jason appeared less deathly pale and sweaty.

"Okay, we're off," Trevor finally announced, and they wheeled Jason into the corridor.

Once out of the room, Kelly could hear the rapper droning away and shouts from the crowd. Weird to think they were blissfully unaware of the drama unfolding backstage. The kid with the cap and the low-crotch trousers who'd introduced Kelly on stage was hovering outside.

"You all right, Miss … Kelly?" he asked.

"I've been better, Kayden. But thanks."

Kelly couldn't believe she'd come up with his name. Especially since it was one of those hybrid ones people dream up, thinking they're being all original and creative, but their poor kids have to spell it out every day of their lives until they give up and change it to John or Susan — anything, as long as they'll never have to explain it again. She didn't know what came over her when she kissed him, a good wet plonker on his cheek. He just looked so caring and concerned — exactly what she needed at that moment.

When the girl with tattoos and more piercings than Kelly would have believed possible on her face and ears held open the door to the Catacomb, Kelly heard a few indecipherable shouts and muffled exclamations outside.

When she followed the gurney out to the ambulance, which was mercifully at the kerb close to the club entrance, a gaggle of camera-wielding paps pounced on the group, shutters going off as frenetic as firecrackers on bonfire night. Kelly turned, but Donovan seemed to have made himself scarce. Just as well, or she swore to God she'd have killed the little bastard. It was obvious to her he'd phoned these parasites from inside the club. How else could they have known?

"Sling your hooks, the lot of you," yelled Trevor, the bulky paramedic. He stood arms outstretched, his massive frame protecting his partner as she hefted the gurney onto its tracks and into the ambulance. Kelly hopped in before any of the paps could reach around Trevor's hefty bulk. The last thing she saw from inside was him pushing a photographer in the chest with one hand while slamming the ambulance door closed with his other. He was around the ambulance and into the driver's seat with a speed Kelly wouldn't have thought possible in such a large man. Tracey sat at Jason's head, reaching over occasionally to poke the machine he was hooked up to. As they pulled away, flashes could be seen through the dark glass of the back doors. Frigging paps, so desperate to get a shot they'd take a photo of the back of a bloody ambulance, thought Kelly.

She found the rocking movement of the ambulance and Tracey's quiet presence oddly calming. It was only then she realized neither of the paramedics had shown any sign that they knew who she was. Kelly found their apparent ignorance of her fame — or notoriety — comforting. What did it say about her life that their indifference to her made the frigging horror show of Jason's overdose seem normal? Almost like it was an everyday event happening to ordinary people — her and Jason. But, no matter how much Kelly might have wished differently, she was painfully aware they weren't ordinary people, and this wasn't an everyday event.

"Which hospital are we going to?" she asked.

"Dispatch gave us a choice — St Thomas' or Chelsea and Westminster. We took St Thomas'."

"Is there a back door?" Kelly asked, but she already knew the answer.

Tracey smiled.

"Not as such, but if there are any of those leeches in front of A&E, we'll have you inside before they can lift a camera, let alone take a photo. Trev will see to that."

She studied Kelly, as if to make sure she'd been reassuring enough. Then, as though she somehow doubted herself, she said, "But I expect you're used to it."

So, they'd known who she was all along. Kelly had been stupid to think otherwise. Despondency hit her so unexpectedly she couldn't hold back tears.

"Hey, it's okay," said Tracey. "He's gonna be fine. He'll likely have a stonking great headache, but that should be all."

As if to add to the paramedic's reassurance, Jason let out a low moan and moved his head. He opened his eyes briefly.

"Wha' ... fuck ...," he muttered. He pushed at the gurney with his feet, as though trying to raise himself.

"Lie still, Jason," said Tracey. "You're going to be okay. Just don't try to move or talk. You'll feel better that way."

She glanced over at Kelly as if to say, 'Come on then, reassure him.' But Kelly felt antsy seeing Jason incapacitated. She wanted him strong and cocky, the way he always was. She summoned up the nerve to reach for his hand. Despite being moist and cool — Jason's hands were always warm and dry — he gripped her fingers so strongly that Kelly almost cried out. She'd always been a bit in awe of him, although she really liked him, obviously. And he turned her on like nobody else. But she'd never felt anything like the strength of affection for him that hit her when he clasped her hand so needfully. She was almost ashamed when the thought hit her that this was exactly the kind of quirky situation that would make a great song. Love blossoming in the back of an ambulance after an overdose. Would she remember what it felt like? But then she realized a more telling question would be: how would she ever come up with words to describe it?

Despite Trevor's best efforts to shield Kelly and the gurney from the couple of photographers waiting at the entrance to A&E, Kelly was certain the bastards had bagged more than a few shots before they were whisked inside. She recognized one of them as having been outside the Catacomb. So, there was truth to the 'ambulance-chaser' label. Thank Christ a couple of security guards stopped the paps at the doors. But then, even though Jason's gurney was off to one side behind another patient waiting to be admitted, Kelly had to endure the obvious stares, nudges, and whispers of people waiting in reception. Several moved closer for a better view. A weedy guy wearing an old Stranglers T-shirt edged towards Kelly, his device up to his face, obviously filming with a new smart phone.

"Screw triage, we'll do it inside," said Trevor. He and Tracey whisked the gurney past the one ahead of them, almost colliding with an astonished nurse holding a clipboard. They crashed through some double doors, and into the inner sanctum of the emergency department. Trouble was, they couldn't have advertised Kelly's arrival better if they'd done a drum roll. The speed and sound of their arrival had everyone — and there were a lot of them — staring in their direction. Even an old guy in the nearest bed, who looked like he was about to gasp his last breath, lifted his head to look.

There was a moment when Kelly felt as if the world had stopped, like the game she used to play as a kid when everybody had to freeze, and then, if one of them moved, they were 'it'. She racked her brains to think how it was you made them all move again. Exasperated, she was on the verge of screaming, "What the fuck are you all looking at?" when Trevor, bless him, started spouting medical jargon about Jason to a tall guy in blue scrubs, who Kelly assumed was a doctor.

"Twenty-seven-year-old male. Suspected drug overdose, crack cocaine. BP: one hundred over seventy. No cardiopulmonary arrest but minor hypoxemia, oxygen administered. Five milligram diazepam administered."

It worked like magic. Everybody in Emergency continued with whatever it was they'd been doing.

"Right, let's get him in and check him out," said the tall doctor. "And we need to catheterize him pronto."

A nurse ushered them all, Kelly included, into a compartment and pulled the curtains.

After Trevor and Tracey lifted Jason off the gurney and onto a bed, the nurse undressed him astonishingly quickly. She had a catheter in and a gown on him almost before Kelly knew what was happening. The doctor appeared and whipped out his stethoscope. He bent over Jason, who moaned. Kelly presumed it was at the touch of cold metal on his chest.

"You're okay Mr. ..." The doctor hesitated.

"Jason Campbell," said Trevor. He smiled at Kelly and made a move to wheel the gurney out of the cubicle.

"Thanks," said Kelly. "Really, thanks a lot." She wanted to hug Trevor, but something about his uniform, or the situation, prevented her. That, and a look in his eyes she hardly recognized. But then it struck her. It was pity. Nobody had looked at her like that since she was a kid. Probably one of her disapproving teachers, except with them the pity was always tinged with a good dose of judgement. Trevor was definitely not judging her, she'd have known. She gazed at him in astonishment for a split second before Tracey, the other paramedic, approached her from the other side of the bed.

"Kelly, I hope you don't mind, but my brother's mental about you. Could you just sign, 'Love to Chris.'"

She thrust a ball-point pen and a piece of paper, some kind of printed form, in front of Kelly.

Trevor frowned and gave his partner a dirty look, before he continued to wheel the gurney out of the compartment. Kelly wanted to beg him not to leave, but she just took the piece of paper from Tracey and scrawled the message on it together with her signature. Kelly stared at the powder blue curtain after it fell back into place behind the two paramedics, but all she saw in her mind's eye was the expression of pity in Trevor's eyes.

"*F*OR THE LOVE of Allah, get them all on memory sticks. We need more back-ups than on a footie team," said Ali.

Frank didn't know what to question first: Ali's invocation of Allah, which he suspected was highly blasphemous, or the lad's obvious ignorance of football in calling subs 'back-ups.' He decided to keep quiet, realizing Ali's initial relief and subsequent euphoria over downloading a good selection of perfect shots from Rashid's spectacles had quickly morphed into a terror of somehow losing them.

"Chill, man. We still got them all on memory in the glasses, innit," said Rashid.

"But you can never have too much back-up when they's so rarefied," said Ali.

As soon as all images were downloaded onto a memory stick, Frank insisted he alone go through them on the laptop.

"No offence lads, but I can tell in a heartbeat what's

going to ring a photo editor's chimes and what isn't."

Despite Frank's stipulation that he be the one to choose, Ali nudged his chair right up to Frank's so he could oversee the editing process. Frank could smell his breath. Not unpleasant. Slightly sweet, from the lemon and lime pop he'd been drinking, and a hint of the sugar-coated aniseeds the lad was constantly popping into his mouth.

Frank quickly narrowed the shots down to three. He was relieved when he received no argument from Ali. One was a straight shot from early on, with Kelly looking totally majestic, singing the song that that had affected Frank so much. One of her staring at the camera, obviously frozen with fear after she lost the plot and stopped singing. And a final snap of her moving off-stage, distress etched into her face. Frank couldn't believe how clear they were. He wondered if maybe it was just as well that he'd been forced out of the business. If any Tom, Dick, or Ali could so easily snap shots of this quality, the days of the paparazzi were definitely numbered. It wouldn't be long 'til the web would be flooded with celeb pictures taken by amateurs, devaluing any that a pap could take.

"Over to you Ali. Superimpose the watermark you made onto low-res versions so they can't use them, and then send the buggers off to that e-mail list of publications I gave you, pronto."

Frank had earlier drafted an e-mail to various photo editors around town asking for best price for total buy-out of each photo offered. He and Ali didn't have the time or resources to mess around with single-use fees. Frank was familiar with all the editors who'd be working at that hour, putting their papers or magazines to bed. And he was aware of the ones who were constantly updating their web sites. Frank had quickly added a brief description to the e-mail about Kelly's surprise appearance at the Catacomb. He knew some wanker of an editor or writer would be quick to insinuate that Kelly's freakout was down to drugs, but he remembered her expression and demeanour, more of terror than inebriation. He was damned if he was going to describe her as high or trashed in any way. He just said that she'd 'broken down'. Everybody the e-mail was sent to was given an hour to respond. Then Frank would take the highest price and Ali would send high-res originals with no watermark. After that, the customer could do whatever the hell they wished with the image.

"Shall we push the boat out and have another drink while we're waiting?" asked Frank. He couldn't really afford to buy a round, but he was counting on having some extra cash from the sale of the photos. And he figured it was the least he could do, especially for Rashid, who didn't stand to make anything from his efforts.

"Yeah, go on then," said Rashid.

"Two lemon and limes, and a diet Coke, please," said Frank to a barman with a florid face. There was nobody else working so Frank assumed he must be the publican. The place carried a distinct air of disuse. There'd only been half-a-dozen other customers all evening. The room wasn't noticeably shabby but had none of the spit and polish Frank had seen in more lively establishments. Frank had told Ali he was surprised the pub had wifi. Ali looked puzzled and said, "What kind of a place wouldn't have wifi?"

"Six pound fifty," said the man as he pushed the drinks across the bar.

It seemed like a small fortune to Frank, but he could imagine what the publican was thinking by the sour expression on his ruddy face — that two Muslims and a recovering alcoholic weren't exactly going to finance his retirement in Mallorca. Not even a caravan park in Bognor, come to that.

"Cheers," said Frank, as he plonked some pound coins and a fifty pence piece on the bar.

The publican ignored him. He scooped up the money with one sweep of his hand.

"Why in't no-one got back to us?" asked Ali, peering at his laptop.

"Give 'em a chance, it's only been ten minutes," said Frank.

He sipped his diet Coke and tried to think of some way to distract his young workmate.

"So, if you gents weren't here, what would you have been up to this evening?" he asked.

Ali looked at Frank like he was a space alien, but at least he averted his gaze from the laptop.

"We'd probably be gaming at mine," said Rashid.

Frank noticed a slight frown flit across Ali's brow.

"Yeah, I'm sometimes at Rash's 'cos he's got an X-box," said Ali.

This time it was Rashid's turn to frown.

"Sometimes?" he said, looking at Ali. Somewhat accusingly, thought Frank.

Ali looked at Rashid and frowned again. Frank thought he saw an accompanying shake of his head. Just at that moment the laptop pinged.

"E-mail!" shouted Ali. Frank noticed the publican look up from reading his Evening Standard and scowl.

"Whassis? This wanker's havin' a laugh. Five hundred pounds for the three. That can't be right, can it, Frank?"

Frank swivelled the laptop so he could read the e-mail. It was from the MailOnline and Ali was right, all they were offering was five hundred pounds. Frank couldn't believe it. The MailOnline was massive, they should have been offering five thousand each, not five hundred the lot. There was a second sentence after the offer saying they wanted the shots to accompany "the main story."

"Main story?" Frank said out loud. "What main story?"

"What they on about, Frank?" asked Ali.

"Lend me your phone," said Frank.

He phoned the number at the bottom of the e-mail and reached the photo editor directly, a man he vaguely remembered from his time at the Mail.

"Listen, Terry," said Frank. "What's this pathetic offer. You're gonna have to do a lot better than that. You're the second most-visited site in the world, for fuck's sake."

"Who is this?" asked Terry.

In the heat of the moment Frank had forgotten that he hadn't put his name to the e-mails, not wanting to be traced back to the photos.

"Oh sorry, mate. It's Ali, Ali ... erm ... Kwaju. I sent you some Kelly Anton photos."

"Kha-wa-ja," said Ali in a fierce stage whisper. But by then Terry was talking.

"Oh yeah. They're good, but too bad you didn't bag the main event."

"What are you talking about, the main event?" asked Frank.

Ali was by then so close to Frank's ear, trying to hear the conversation, Frank could feel the heat from his face.

"The overdose and that," said Terry.

"What fucking overdose?"

"Kelly's wanker of a boyfriend, Jason Campbell. He O/D-ed in the club while she was on stage. Ambulance called, the lot. He didn't die, unfortunately. But we snagged some brilliant shots of him on a stretcher looking very fucking rough, with Kelly Anton bent over him. And of her getting in the ambulance looking stricken. And of them going in the hospital. We paid a shit load for them. So that price for yours is the best I can do. We only want them for background."

"It should be single use for that amount. Rights revert back to us."

"Piss off," said Terry. "We can easily use old shots of

Kelly Anton out of her skull from our archive. Just thought it'd be nice to have ones from the actual club where her fella O/D-ed, but …"

"Let me call you back," said Frank.

"Don't take all night, Ali," said Terry. "Or we won't want them at all."

"Five minutes at most," said Frank and rang off.

"What did he say? What's going on?" asked Ali.

Frank filled Ali and Rashid in on the overdose and the fact that there were shots of it floating around.

"You wouldn't think they'd give a shit about Jason whassis name," said Rashid.

"'Cos he's Kelly Anton's boyfriend and she was there with him, it's a huge story," said Frank. "So basically, we've been scooped … big time."

Ali put his head in his hands and groaned. Rashid looked concerned and put a comforting hand on Ali's arm.

"Give me a minute," said Frank. "I might have an idea."

It wasn't the first time he'd had exclusive photos in the bag only to find they weren't quite as valuable as he'd thought. Figuring what to do next was all part of the game, and when a bit of cunning had to be called upon. If Terry had paid a "shit load," as he put it, for the ambulance and hospital shots, he'd obviously paid for exclusive rights. There couldn't have been more than a couple of paps who just happened to be close enough when they picked up on the emergency-services phone line they'd obviously been listening in on. How else could they have known about Jason's overdose? Which would mean there might only be one other lot of photos floating around at most, which by then had probably been sold to the next best player to MailOnline. One of the dailies, or even an American web site.

"Okay," said Frank. "Here's what we do."

The two lads looked up.

"I'll call and tell MailOnline we're on for the five hundred."

"What?" said Ali. "Are you insane?"

"You get on the phone to as many of the smaller fish as possible, the ones we didn't e-mail. Metro for one. With a bit of luck, they won't have any shots of the overdose because the big boys will have snapped them all up. They'll be gagging for something else to run with the story. Offer them shots of Kelly in the club where Jason O/D-ed. Take whatever they offer. If we hustle, we can still make a few grand."

"But aren't we selling exclusive-rights to MailOnline?" said Ali.

The lad was smart, but not devious enough, thought Frank.

"You nabbed at least twenty photos, right? We won't sell the exact same shot twice," said Frank. "But if we can sell a few slightly different versions, we'll do okay. Editors won't like it, but screw 'em. Make sure to stipulate the shots are not to run with any credit, okay? No name of the photographer. You don't want to start your career as a paparazzo with a reputation for fiddling people on the exclusive rights thing."

"Who said I wanted a career as a papa-fucking-razzo?" said Ali.

"Or we can just go for the five hundred from MailOnline," said Frank. "I'm easy."

"All right, all right. Let's do it," said Ali.

By the time the publican lustily called last orders — obviously relieved that the evening was finally drawing to a close — they'd sold seven more shots to various publications and web sites, for a total of around four thousand pounds. Rashid turned out to be the lynchpin in the operation, scouring Google for contact numbers and e-mail addresses on his laptop. He even rooted out a couple of trashy French and German web sites who'd paid over the odds at a thousand euros for each photo. Frank thought that, once he was in a position to digitize his vast cache of transparencies, he'd be all over Rashid to be his salesperson, if he wasn't a Silicon Valley billionaire by then.

"So, with the measly five hundred from MailOnline, and supposing the euro doesn't tank, we should pull in six thousand and eighty-two quid," said Ali. "Not exactly the riches I'd been promised."

"I seem to remember mentioning five grand at the low end, and we've topped that, so stop whining."

"Not too shabby, innit," said Rashid.

Frank recognized the shine in Rashid's eyes as the excitement he'd felt in the early days, when he first started peddling his paparazzo pics. How long had it taken before healthy brilliance had become a jaundiced gleam? Two years? A year? Less?

"We'll make twenty-five hundred each, and give the change to Rashid," he said.

"Brilliant! Thanks, Frank," said Rashid.

"He certainly earned it," said Ali. He winked at Rashid, who grinned back at his friend, obviously delighted.

Something about their exchange made Frank feel awkward, as if he didn't belong. He didn't think it was a racial thing — the white bloke not understanding some kind of Pakistani nuance —but he couldn't put his finger on what it was exactly.

"I'm off," he announced, immediately regretting that he sounded gruff.

"Where's the fire?" asked Ali. An expression he often used if Frank was rushed. "We're leaving too, but first I got something for you."

Ali reached into the leather shoulder bag he called his 'man bag' and pulled out a mobile phone. Frank was confused. Ali's phone was lying on the table. Why did he need another?

"I got this for you," said Ali. "We can't have you living in the last bloody century."

He held the phone out to Frank.

"Take it then. It won't bloody bite."

Frank gingerly took the phone.

"I can't take this," he said.

"Look Frank, it's just a cheapie, stupid, not smart. And it's pay-as-you-go. I loaded it up. So, unless you suddenly go wild calling all your celebrity friends around the world, you won't need to top it up for a while."

Frank didn't know what to say.

"Just take it Frank," said Rashid. "He can't stand the thought of not being able to reach you any time he wants. It's a control thing."

"Control, my arse," said Ali. "Grown man ought to have a phone, innit."

Frank's concern that he might cry kept actual tears out of his eyes. Nevertheless, he couldn't look at Ali for fear he'd lose it.

"Thanks, Ali, I really appreciate it."

"Like I said, you gotta start livin' like it's 2011."

Outside the pub they said their goodbyes somewhat awkwardly. The intimacy of their evening of collaboration — its intensity — meant that the usual "see you later" seemed inadequate. Ali shook Frank's hand, something he'd never done, even when they were first introduced. He averted his eyes, but muttered a heartfelt, "Thanks, Frank." Rashid followed suit but was unable to leave it at that and embraced Frank with his free hand in the kind of distant hug that men gave when a full bear hug might seem over the top. They went in different directions, but after several paces Frank looked back at the two friends. Rashid had his arm draped around Ali's shoulders. It dawned on Frank the reason for the sense of alienation he'd felt earlier, when Ali and Rashid were smiling at each other, eyes literally sparkling. For a few seconds he'd been an actual wallflower. The third wheel in the presence of two lovers. Frank was quick to realize his fears for Ali's apparent lack of any life outside of staring at a computer screen were totally unfounded. What a condescending tosser he'd been. He felt glad for Ali, though.

When Kelly stepped out of the private lift and into the hallway of her penthouse, she could still see in her mind's eye the image of Trevor the paramedic's expression of pity. The look on his face had been on her mind all the time she'd stood, gazing out of the window in Jason's hospital room, wondering if he'd ever wake up.

The glossy pamphlet she'd been given by the hospital when she opted for a private room for Jason boasted, 'Our Westminster Unit not only offers world-class medical facilities in comfortable surroundings but also some of the best views in London. Our private rooms look out across the river Thames offering an unrivalled panorama that includes many of the city's famous landmarks.' Kelly had to admit the sight of the illuminated parliament buildings, lying directly across the river, was spectacular, but it seemed somehow wrong to her that the NHS was using the view as a lure to pull in private patients. She'd been under the impression that privatization of the health care service hadn't happened yet, but, judging from the brochure, a two-tier system was obviously already firmly in place. She couldn't help bridling at the idea. She blamed her staunchly socialist mother for that. She'd drilled into Kelly the importance of a welfare state. She wouldn't be too happy if she knew Kelly was shelling out for a private hospital room. Kelly thought about phoning her — not to tell her mother about paying, but to reassure her that she and Justin were okay. Kelly guessed they might have made the news already. But it was too late, her mother would be in bed. And anyway, if her father answered there'd be hell to pay. She came close to tears when she thought about how, after the night's event, there was no way she'd ever persuade him that Justin wasn't a hopeless crackhead.

"Doesn't Big Ben keep everybody awake?" Kelly asked the nurse when she came in to check on Jason just as the unmistakable sounds of the massive bell announced the midnight hour. The nurse laughed and said that patients did sometimes complain.

"I tell them Big Ben chiming every hour, day and night, is what got Britain through World War II, but most couldn't give a toss," said the nurse.

Kelly could well imagine the type of clients who'd demand the bell be silenced. Assholes who considered themselves rich enough for the whole world to be at their beck and call.

"I wish Big Ben would bleeding well wake Jason up," she said.

"Why don't you go home, get some sleep?" said the nurse. "He's stable. Probably won't wake now 'til morning."

Having received permission of sorts, Kelly had left, somewhat reluctantly. She was relieved to see a solitary waiting taxi and dashed to it from the front doors of the hospital. But she needn't have worried, there was no sign of any photographers. Kelly supposed they'd all pissed off to sell their misbegotten goods to the parasites in the press. She hoped her twinge of disappointment at not seeing them was about her being dog tired and delirious rather than being so fucked in the head she missed the attention. Probably a bit of both. As her taxi had sped along the deserted south bank and the few silent streets to her building, she'd tried not to think about what she might look like in whatever shots had been snapped.

Kelly's heels echoed around the penthouse as she crossed a sea of polished wood floor to the kitchen, the area nearest the wall of glass to the north-east. She could smell the toast she'd made just before they left for the gig. She liked it a little charred, so she had the toaster turned up to its highest setting. The odour of scorched bread almost overpowered the faint but pervasive smell of crack. The place reeked whenever Jason fired up, but the stench soon dissipated. Trouble was, it left a tenacious trace, as if some plastic had recently been burnt. Kelly had heard there was a trick to cutting the stink, something about smoking it in a steamy bathroom. Jason had given her a withering look when she suggested he try it. She thrust open the double doors to the terrace, took a step outside and inhaled supposedly fresh air.

Maybe she should have listened to Donovan and bought a house with windows she could open, even if it would let in London air, which Kelly didn't believe was as polluted as they claimed. She sometimes wondered when it was that she'd become so sceptical. Maybe when she started to read news reports about herself. They always got everything wrong, so how was she supposed to believe anything else she read? And if she could so easily get them to say what she wanted, it must be a doddle for others to do the same.

She stood, relishing the sensation of a light breeze on her face, taking measured, deep breaths. But her enjoyment was spoilt when the memory of Trevor, the paramedic's, expression came back to her. What gave him the right to pity her, anyway? Kelly thought resentfully. It might look to him like her life being hounded by paparazzi was shit, but he didn't know the half of it. The fact that she had audiences — big fucking audiences — to play her music to, was worth all the hassles, wasn't it?

Then she remembered her present dilemma. She grimaced. If she didn't see her way to some lyrics for a new album soon there wouldn't be any performances, nor any paps to contend with, they'd have lost interest before she knew it. She'd be lucky if she could even get a gig back at the Cobden Club. As Kelly gazed out over a motionless cityscape of twinkling lights, just the odd car headlight tracing its way between avenues of yellow or orange streetlamps, she wished she could explain her problems to someone. It'd be such a relief to get the whole shebang — the reason for her lack of material and Donovan's stupid scheme — off her chest. She hadn't even explained things properly to Jason, for fuck's sake. She supposed she was worried he'd think she'd made a balls-up, dragging him through the mud for no good reason. But, man, it was lonely, carrying it all around. A burden that seemed to grow heavier by the day.

She wondered if she might be looking out to where Trevor or Tracey lived. One of them could be in a grotty rental over there in West Kensington. Or, if they were lucky, they each had a cramped flat in a shared ownership block, maybe across the river in Chelsea or up in Highbury. Her mother had banged on about the developments being one of the few good ideas of government because they allowed essential services people — police, firefighters, nurses, and the like — to stay in Central London where they were needed but couldn't otherwise afford to live.

It was weird to think of the thousands and thousands of people below her, all asleep in their beds. Weirder still to think they'd almost all know her name. And really fucked up to think that many of them might think they knew Kelly Anton as well as they knew their best friends. She wondered if she'd ever get used to the idea that thousands and thousands of people knew who she was. That thought always creeped her out.

99

She shivered slightly and turned to look in the direction of the City to the east. She could plainly see office towers stacked with brightly lit floors, each one probably as deserted as the Mary Celeste, the ship she'd been so intrigued by as a kid. The fact that it was found intact except for its missing crew fascinated her. What a blast to be able to disappear like that, without a trace.

An expanse of darkness marked Hampstead Heath to the north, giving Kelly the impression that a large black blanket had been thrown over that section of the city.

When she stepped back inside, she could tell the breeze had freshened the penthouse. All she could smell was a faint suggestion of burnt toast and maybe the merest whiff of crack. She stripped off and fell into bed in just her pants. She missed Jason and hoped to hell he was okay. She curled up into a ball, the way she always slept when she was alone and exhausted. But sleep evaded her. Every time she drifted off, she was jerked awake by the feeling — or maybe it was a nightmare — that she was back in the Catacomb looking out at the crowd and completely panicked that she was losing them with her new song. The melodrama with Jason had temporarily pushed aside thoughts of her performance, but now, lying in the semi-darkness of her bed, London's glow reflecting off her ceiling, she couldn't escape the memory of it.

She turned several times until, in a fit of frustration, she punched Jason's pillow ferociously. Not that her anger was aimed at him. It was her father she was pummelling. All the blame could be laid at his door — for the performance anxiety, for her 'drought,' the lot. He was so stubborn, it made Kelly mental. Although her mother would have said they were often as bad as each other. "You need your heads banging together," she muttered.

To make matters worse she could hear her father's voice, "You overtired, gyal. You need tek some rest." The belittling words he always came up with to put her down when she expressed any of her frustration with him. Which of course sent her into paroxysms of rage. It hadn't always been so. Up until Jason, everything had been storybook happy. She adored her father, and he loved his little girl. It seemed to Kelly that her growing into a full-grown, sexually active woman was impossible for him to accept.

"It all stems from those years he was lost."

That's how her mother described the period, before Kelly was born, when she and Nelson had split up for a few years. Lost. As if he'd forgotten the way home one day, then wandered around aimlessly for months on end before stumbling across their house again quite by accident.

"He's never told me the full story, but he was up to all kind of tricks," said Kelly's mother. "I know some of them involved drugs. That's why he's so dead set against them. You can't blame your Dad for not wanting his daughter to live with a crackhead, as pleasant as he might appear." No matter how much she insisted Jason wasn't an addict, they never believed her. And who could blame them, given the stories in the press.

On the few occasions when they'd first met him, Jason had been his usual charming public-schoolboy self. Not that he was insincere, he was genuinely interested in them. Kelly could tell her mother suspected him of condescension, with his plummy accent. And her father once asked Jason outright. "Yuh sure you want hear 'bout Jamaica?" he said, when Jason pushed him about what it was like growing up there. After Jason insisted that he did, Nelson had seemed willing to assign Jason's family's slave connection to history. Things were going well until the first bad press, and then there was the smell of crack her father had detected on Jason's clothes.

"For why yuh smell like burning plastic?" he'd asked, eyes narrowed.

Kelly punched the pillow again. It seemed like sleep became more elusive with each night. And always, there at the edge of Kelly's consciousness, or sometimes centre stage in her head, was the realization that sooner rather than later Donovan would call a halt to their scheme to explain away her lack of material and expect her to come up with some songs. Then what would she do?

After FRANK HAD left Ali and Rashid and as his bus juddered over Chelsea Bridge and made its way through the shadowy streets of Battersea, Frank's mind went back time and again to something that Terry, the MailOnline photo editor, had said earlier that evening.

"Jason Campbell. He O/D-ed in the club. He didn't die, *unfortunately.*"

It was the editor's disgruntled emphasis on the word 'unfortunately' that niggled Frank. He hadn't picked up on it at the time, yet he'd known exactly what the word, and Terry's tone, had implied. If Jason had kicked the bucket in the club or in the ambulance, it would have been cause for exultation in the Mail's newsroom, knowing they'd snagged exclusive photos of him dead or dying. As it was, they must have known he'd survived. Probably paid off someone inside the hospital who'd told them that Jason was still in the land of the living.

Frank never forgot what the gnarled photo editor at the Mail had once told him when he first started working there, "Never underestimate the public's thirst for the macabre." Pictures of Kelly Anton bent over her dying, or already dead, boyfriend would have meant back slapping, wide grins, and raucous drinks in the pub that night for staff at the Mail. Because exclusive shots like that would have meant beating the competition with a shitload more papers sold, and millions more hits on the MailOnline web site — which was all that mattered at the end of the day.

Thinking about Terry's "unfortunately" comment, Frank experienced slight nausea accompanied by an increase in saliva. He swallowed and breathed heavily and purposefully to rid himself of the sensation that he might throw up. He remembered that he'd experienced a similar sensation after he walked away from the devastation of the 7/7 terrorist bombing in Tavistock Square. Except then he couldn't stop himself from puking. At the time Frank had presumed it was just shock from being a witness to the bloodbath.

When he heard the bomb blast, he'd been door-stepping at a hotel just down the street, on the strength of a tip-off from the receptionist that Mickey Rourke was staying there. Sin City had just been released and magazines were paying generously for up-to-date snaps of Rourke after his big Hollywood comeback. Frank was waiting for the actor to leave the hotel that morning, when he heard the explosion. He hadn't known it was a bomb, but even if it was something as innocent as a gas leak, he knew from the thunderous sound that photos of whatever had happened were sure to be saleable. As he ran up Woburn Place, he never dreamt he'd be confronted by the ghastly carnage that lay ahead.

Frank had known that putting his viewfinder to his eye was as much about shielding himself from the scene as it was about taking photographs. He was well aware his camera would act as a buffer between him and the dead, dying, and injured commuters strewn around a mass of contorted metal that used to be a bus. As soon as he had people in frame — a writhing man with a missing leg, a woman in a blood-soaked shirt standing stock-still in shock, a young girl sitting on a kerb sobbing — Frank became inured to the horror.

All that concerned him was the quality of the photo: how well it was composed; was he close enough; was it better to use vertical versus horizontal format. God help him, he'd even felt a kind of thrill when he snagged a particularly gruesome shot. One he knew that photo editors would jump at. A picture for which they'd pay good money — and they did. Frank made a bundle from his Tavistock Square photos. The bloodiest ones had earned him the most money. But later, he couldn't escape the thought that he could have put down his camera and tried to help. He imagined himself leading the woman who'd been standing, bloodied and in shock, to somebody who could help her. He could have comforted the sobbing girl on the kerb. Even staunched the flow of blood from someone's wound. Frank cringed at the memory. He gazed out at darkened side streets and tried his best not to look at his own murky face reflected in the bus window.

The walk from the bus stop took him past a pub at the corner of his street. When Frank pushed on a polished brass handle next to a frosted glass door panel etched with a floral motif, there was no debate in his head, no conscious decision. It was as though he was merely a puppet and some higher force was pulling his strings. The pub was crowded and noisy, customers were two- and three-deep at the bar. The devil on his shoulder was whispering, "What's the harm in one? It's all you'll be able to have anyway. They'll be closing soon." But another voice deeper inside Frank was saying, "But you know you can always buy a bottle, take it back to your place." Not a warning kind of voice, but one that carried a reassuring tone, as if to say, "go right ahead, there's more if you want it." And, even though he knew damn well that he'd want it, he nevertheless pushed his way closer to the bar.

The two harried barmen were filling orders. It was clear customers were hurrying to get in last drinks before the place closed. Frank was beginning to feel panicky. What if they closed before he could order? He shoved the man next to him so he could edge closer to the bar.

"Watch who you're pushing," the man said, glaring at Frank.

"Sorry," said Frank, but he wasn't. He was in a zone entirely on his own, totally consumed with the idea of a drink — just one, honest.

Elbows now on the polished wooden bar, Frank assumed the expectant, pleading expression of a person anxious to be served. Then, for a split-second, Frank thought the bloke he'd shoved had electrocuted him, or maybe stabbed him in the leg. What the fuck was that sharp vibration on his thigh? Then he heard the ring, like the bell of an old-fashioned phone. Frank fished the phone that Ali had given him out of the trouser pocket where he'd stashed it. By some miracle he pressed the right button and when he put the phone to his ear, he heard Ali's voice.

"Brilliant ring tone, or what?"

"Yeah," said Frank. "Yeah, clever."

"What's yours?" one of the busy barmen asked Frank. Frank froze.

"Where are you?" asked Ali in Frank's ear.

"Come on mate, we haven't got all night," said the barman.

"Packet of crisps, please. Salt and vinegar, if you've got them," said Frank.

The barman rolled his eyes, leaned over and ripped a packet off a rack hanging to one side of the bar, and threw it in front of Frank.

"Are you in a fucking pub?" asked Ali.

Frank paid for his crisps and fought his way to the door.

"Yeah, I was starving so dropped in for some crisps," Frank told Ali, as he burst out into the street.

"You know those things are poison, right? All the stuff

they process them with, not to mention the pesticides in the sodding potatoes they use."

Frank was gasping at cool air as desperate and urgent as somebody who's almost drowned.

"I know but needs must. I had nothing at home, and I was desperate."

"Hmm," said Ali. "Well I just wanted to test your phone, innit. See you tomorrow."

And with that he rung off. Frank stared at the phone for several seconds before pushing a red button, in the hopes it was the right thing to do. The whole episode of being in the pub seemed like a dream, or a nightmare. Frank turned and walked, zombie-like, slowly down his street.

He'd learned by listening to other recovering alcoholics at meetings, that they almost always had some underlying reason for drinking. Maybe there was some kind of genetic biological tendency to their alcoholism, which is why some medication could take away the urge to drink, but you could bet some experience would have triggered it in the first place. He was well aware later, but not at the time, that he'd started drinking more and more after his Tavistock Square bombing experience. Given his reaction earlier after he'd thought about the photo editor's 'unfortunately' comment — the sensation that he might puke — Frank wondered if he might have post-traumatic stress from the 7/7 bloodshed and mayhem he'd seen. But Frank's natural scepticism clicked in and he dismissed the idea, just like he dismissed the God element in the AA Twelve Step programme. He just took from it what he needed and left the religious aspect to those that depended on it.

In his heart of hearts Frank suspected that the nauseous reaction he'd experienced was born out of disgust at himself for once having been no better than the MailOnline photo editor, lusting after the grisliest image possible. He supposed maybe he'd drunk to escape that aspect of himself. It was a better reason than most he could think of.

When Frank reached home, he threw the packet of crisps on the table, pulled off his clothes and fell into bed. He escaped into sleep before his head hit the pillow.

"ALL YOU HAD to do is ask, you know," said Jason as soon as Kelly walked into his hospital room. He was sitting on the bed, fully clothed, waiting for her to pick him up. "No need to slip me a date-rape drug."

Kelly frowned. She looked at the nurse for a clue.

"What's he on about?"

The nurse glanced at Jason who nodded.

"Tell her. She won't believe it coming from me," he said.

"Tests were carried out on Jason's urine and blood," said the nurse. "We test for various drugs other than what the patients say they've taken. It's standard procedure, just to be sure. Jason tested positive for Rohypnol."

"Fucking date-rape drug, Kelly," said Jason. "The minute I woke up this morning and they told me what had happened, I knew it wasn't an overdose. You know how careful I am. I make certain the stuff's clean, and I never go overboard. When have I ever even come close to O/D-ing?"

Kelly stared at him as the insane fact sank in.

"You don't really think it was me give it to you?"

"No, I was just teasing you, sweetheart," said Jason.

"It could have been serious," said the nurse. "The paramedics administered diazepam, Valium. It's something we give against possible seizures in cases of crack cocaine overdose. But both Rohypnol and Valium are benzodiazepines, a type of sedative. The two together could conceivably have had fatal consequences, depending on the amount of Rohypnol Jason was given."

Kelly gazed out of the window trying to make sense of what she'd heard. The Houses of Parliament looked further away than they had the night before, when they'd been brightly illuminated. Despite the sunny morning, the sand-coloured buildings were veiled slightly by a light mist rising from the river.

"I can't remember much about being at that club, except it was a dump," said Jason

"Rohypnol wipes memory, sometimes even of the minutes before it's taken," said the nurse. "That's why rapists love it. For obvious reasons."

"They tell me it's usually slipped into someone's drink," said Jason. "But I wasn't drinking, was I?"

Kelly turned from the window to stare at Jason. She didn't like the thought that flowered in her head.

"What?" asked the nurse, who'd obviously picked up something from her expression.

Kelly was too disbelieving of her own logic to answer. But there couldn't be any other explanation.

"What?" said Jason. "What the fuck did I drink?"

"Donovan," said Kelly.

"What about him?"

"He brought us lattes. You drank yours."

It was clear to Kelly that Jason was going through the same thought process that she'd experienced seconds before. His brow furrowed and he looked totally perplexed.

"Donovan? No, he couldn't have."

Kelly raised her eyebrows, opened her eyes wide. An expression to indicate there was no other explanation.

"Why the hell would Donovan slip me a date-rape drug?" said Jason. "He's a weird bastard, but ..."

They hardly spoke in the cab on the way home from the hospital. It was as though they were both too stunned by the Rohypnol revelation to talk. Kelly scoured her thoughts to see if she could make any sense of why, in God's name, Donovan would want Jason drugged up and incoherent. She pictured in her mind the series of events at the Catacomb. Donovan hadn't seemed particularly surprised or shocked when they discovered Jason in the dressing room sprawled out and comatose. When he phoned emergency services, he was cool as a cucumber. But why would he have purposely drugged Jason?

Then she remembered that Donovan had been on the phone twice in the dressing room — once to emergency services and then again after they'd arrived. She'd suspected, once she saw the paps, that it was him who'd called them. How else would they have known about the so-called overdose and been waiting outside the club?

Kelly pulled out her new phone and went straight to the browser. She wasn't one for looking at her own publicity. Like the thoughts she'd had the night before about everyone knowing who she was, her fame more often than not freaked her out. All she'd ever wanted to do was perform songs, and for that she appreciated the attention, but she could do without all the other shit that came with being a 'celebrity.'

Despite her natural reluctance to check out the dross people might be saying, Kelly Googled her name and the word 'overdose'. She punched the top link of a long list. The MailOnline logo popped up and immediately underneath were photos of the whole frigging episode. One of her looking completely freaked alongside the gurney, together with the paramedics, Trevor and Tracey, as they all emerged from the club. A grainy shot, probably taken with a zoom, of Jason's face looking wrecked, his head on the gurney pillow. Then a photo of them going into the hospital through the doors to emergency.

Kelly's inkling of a suspicion grew into almost a certainty. Donovan knew that Jason often carried his crack-in-a-box with him. She had to believe Donovan had given the date-rape drug to Jason, knowing it'd look like an overdose. All so that he could make the most if it with the press. If her theory turned out to be true, Donovan had gone a step too far. Maybe it was time she came clean.

"Do you think Donovan knows you're not a hard-core user?" she asked Jason.

He'd been gazing out of the cab window toward the dense greenery of Battersea Park lining his side of the road. He turned his head, obviously startled.

"I don't know whether to be flattered or insulted that you think I'm not a 'hard core user,' as you put it."

"You know you can go days without touching the stuff, and you said yourself you were always careful."

"I might have once said, when Donovan accused me of fleecing you for drug money, that I had my own bloody money. But then I said, to annoy him, that I'd be asking you for shedloads of cash whenever I became seriously hooked. I think he knew I was joking, but nevertheless he claimed it was inevitable that I'd go that route. But then, when I pointed out that Keith Richards had been taking drugs for years but was never so hooked that he couldn't still pump out a good song, Donovan backed down on his opinion of my eventual demise. So yeah, I suppose he knows I'm not hard core. Why do you ask?"

Kelly agonised whether to tell Jason her theory. It seemed ridiculous, but, given her and Donovan's scheme, she wouldn't discount it altogether. But if she told him, would she have the courage to tell him everything — including her part in Donovan's charade.

"Why," asked Jason again.

"I think it was Donovan's idea of a publicity stunt."

"What do you mean?"

Kelly whipped out her phone and went to the browser, which was still showing the MailOnline page with the photos. She showed Jason.

"I think he drugged you to make it seem like you'd O/D-ed, and then he called the paps to come to the club and grab the photos as we came out."

"But why in God's name would he do that?" asked Jason.

Kelly lost her bottle — there was no way she could tell him the whole story.

"His twisted idea of getting some press, I suppose," she said, eyes lowered.

"Pretty fucked up way to do it," said Jason.

"Yeah," said Kelly, disgusted at herself for not having the guts to come clean.

She was about to turn the phone off when she noticed the top frame of another photo. She scrolled down. What she saw was a photo from inside the club, for fuck's sake. It was either when she was performing her own song, the one that didn't fly, or more likely, during the last number, just before she lost it completely and fled. Seeing the photo brought back the terror-struck, paralyzed feeling she'd had — and, shit, did she look bad. Kelly took in a few words of the caption. 'Anton's star-status tarnished again by drug-addled onstage breakdown …'

Although shaken and angered by the fact that someone had managed to photograph inside the club, Kelly was aware of the high quality of the shot. It was pin sharp. She could see the panic in her eyes, the furrows on her forehead. It was obviously taken within feet of where she'd been standing on the stage. How was it possible after all the fuss about the banning of cameras and phones? Seeing the photo of her looking so wrecked distracted her momentarily from thinking that Donovan had gone too far with this latest stunt. But the thought hit her again that Jason could have died, for fuck's sake.

111

Kelly stared out of the cab window at blocks of mansion flats along Prince of Wales Drive, telling herself she had to work up the courage to tell Jason about her and Donovan's ruse. She promised herself she'd tell him later, once they were back home.

When they arrived at the penthouse it was still early enough for the place to be flooded with sunlight from windows on the east side.

"Christ, it's bright in here," said Jason. He headed for the bedroom area at the western end. "I presume my crack-in-a-box got lost in the brouhaha."

Kelly debated lying. But what was the point? Jason would just send out for more.

"You know what? Sod it," said Jason, before she could say anything. "It's probably not a good idea, and maybe it's time I gave up anyway."

He announced he was off for a shower. A few seconds later Kelly heard the sound of water running in the bathroom. She debated whether or not she should ever give Jason his box, which was still in the pocket of the coat she'd worn the day before. She decided she'd leave it for a while.

Jason's call from the hospital had woken her that morning, and she hadn't had time to clean up before running off to collect him. Kelly pulled off her clothes as she walked across the expanse of polished wood to the bathroom.

Jason's body was bathed in light from the floor-to-ceiling window that made up one side of the huge marble-walled shower area. Kelly had been told the window was one-way glass so no pervert with a telescope in the adjacent building could see in, even if they wanted to. Water streamed from the 'rain forest' shower over Jason's head and shoulders, rivulets ran down his torso. Kelly found it funny that a stream of water ran off his penis making it look as if he was pissing. She stepped into the shower and grasped his dick.

"Jesus, Kelly," said Jason, who'd had his eyes closed.

She put her lips on his mouth, enjoying the sensation of warm shower water on her face, some seeping into her mouth as they kissed more hungrily. It took a few seconds, but Jason was soon well aroused. He pulled her hand away, pushed her against the window and slowly sank to his knees. On the way down he licked her nipple. He took it between his teeth and applied pressure for a second or two, then increased it almost unbearably. Just as she took a sharp intake of breath in anticipation of more intense pain, he released her. He kissed her skin as he slowly worked his way down her body.

After she'd climaxed, clutching Jason's hair while trying her best not to pull it out by the roots, Jason stood and turned her around to face the window. In her post-orgasmic state, the scene beyond seemed dreamlike. Sunlight on the river far below was transformed to a shining strip as it snaked its way towards Westminster. She'd been so admiring of the cityscape below it took her a few seconds to realize Jason had made no effort to bend her over. He merely pressed himself against her back and encircled her with his arms. She turned her head to see his face. He was gazing out of the window.

"You alright?" she asked.

"Yeah," he said, but slowly and unconvincingly.

"What?'

"I can't stop thinking about being taken into hospital for an overdose."

"But it wasn't an overdose," said Kelly, puzzled. "It was Donovan being a psycho idiot."

"I know, but what if it had been, Or, a bad batch. I can't shake the idea that one day it might be."

Kelly had no idea what to say. All she could think was that he was right, it could happen. She pulled his arms around her so that he was hugging her more tightly, but after a moment he pulled away.

"Not in the mood now," he said, frowning. But then he smiled ruefully and said, "That's all I need, for overdose anxiety to mess up my sex drive."

After they'd dried themselves off, Jason collapsed on the bed while Kelly made tea.

"Nothing like a well-brewed cup of tea after cunnilingus," said Jason, exaggerating his plummy posh accent. He slurped on his cup, and grinned.

Kelly scowled in mock disgust. She was well aware some women might find the comment a turn off, but she knew it was just Jason's clumsy way of showing appreciation. She was actually pleased that he seemed a bit more upbeat.

THE FIRST THING Frank remembered when he woke up was how close he'd come to falling off the wagon. Christ! If he'd had the drink he was bent on ordering when he walked into the pub — although it felt more like he was pushed — he dreaded to think what state he'd have been in. He felt shaken up, vulnerable. He'd need to watch himself.

Thank God Ali rang him when he did. Even if Frank had remembered he had the phone, he wouldn't have called his sponsor. He wasn't too keen on the latest one, anyway. A dour Northerner who went along hook, line, and sinker with the religious angle of AA. But why had he come so close?

Frank thought about the events of the previous day. If Jason Campbell had died, and Frank had been in a position to take photos of Kelly with her dead boyfriend, would he have sold them? Just posing the question gave him the sick feeling, saliva pooling in his mouth. He told himself he was being ridiculous. Why ask himself such an unreal question? But he wondered about his reaction when he thought about the money he and Ali had made from the sale of the photos. The fact that he didn't think of the cash in any positive way — not excitedly or pleasantly, but with a dose of disgust — gave him pause. Was there really any harm in selling photos of Kelly Anton in a rough state, whatever had caused it? She hadn't died or anything, just stumbled off a stage.

But then, Frank couldn't shake the thought that maybe he didn't want to sell his cache of photographs after all, valuable as it was. But why not? It wasn't as if every shot showed somebody in distress. Quite the opposite, most were just snaps of famous people doing something totally meaningless, like walking along a street or sitting in a café. And the massive effort involved in digitization wasn't the deterrent. No, it was something less tangible, but overwhelming, nevertheless. Maybe it was Frank's dismay at the colossal number of photos in the world, and the many millions soon to come with the preponderance of smart phones and their amazingly competent built-in cameras. Did he really want to add to the world's vast and unnecessary cache of digital images? Like a kind of massive visual pollution.

But then Frank asked himself if the events of the previous day had rendered him suddenly deranged. Did he want to live in a damp bedsit for the rest of his life? Never be able to afford a anything better? He burrowed deeper in his bed and pulled the covers over his head.

Frank's alarm trilled again, having snoozed for five minutes. He reached out to silence it. The air felt cold on his blanket-warmed head, prompting a flood of more rational, if mundane, thoughts — a quick breakfast, catching the bus, and going to work.

"Some freak called for you just now," said Ali as soon as Frank walked into their basement room at FoodFoto.

"Good morning to you too, Ali," said Frank, relieved that

the slightly awkward bonhomie of the previous evening had given way to Ali's usual abrupt manner.

"Whatever," said Ali and slammed a post-it onto Frank's computer screen.

"No name? Just the number and an extension?"

"The freak said you'd know," said Ali.

"Why do you judge?"

"Wot?"

"The word 'freak.' It's a criticism of sorts."

"He had this squawky voice, innit. Like a cartoon character," said Ali. "Wanker was a bit snippy too. Treated me like the hired help."

Frank resisted pointing out to Ali that they were both 'hired help'. He knew that, at best, it would result in Ali's subservient Pakistani act or, at worst, make him grumpy all day.

Even before the recording on the other end of the phone said, "Welcome to Canary Records," Frank had a suspicion from the familiar phone number and Ali's description that it was Donovan who'd called.

"'ello Frank," said Donovan. It had never occurred to Frank before but, as Ali had implied, his son-in-law's nasal voice was disturbingly similar to Donald Duck's.

"Seems your friend Ali's been a naughty boy."

"Oh yeah?" said Frank, his amusement over Donovan's voice disappearing in a nanosecond.

"There's photos from Kelly Anton's gig last night floating around the internet, and a little bird at MailOnline told me payment for the ones they bought was to a Mr. Ali Ajarwee, your pal what I got passes for."

Given the mangling of Ali's last name, Frank thought about insisting the shots must have come from a different Ali, but he instantly recognized it as a pathetic — and useless — attempt.

"It's Ali Khawaja," he said.

"It could be Ali Baba for all I fucking care," said Donovan.

There were a few seconds of silence. Frank was thinking fast. Thank Christ he'd thought not to have his name linked to any sale of the photos. If he denied all knowledge of the shots, there was little Donovan could do. There was no law to prevent Ali or anyone else taking photos in a dump like the Catacomb. Performers were fair game, and anybody else who was caught in a picture would have to go to a lot of trouble and expense to prove invasion of privacy.

"All I can say is sorry," said Frank. "I had no idea."

"Really?" said Donovan. "Well Frank, you might be surprised to know that your Ali wasn't the only one doing things he shouldn't last night. There's a very fucking clever CCTV camera in the entranceway of that poxy club, what takes video of everyone who goes in and out of the place. And one of the punters on tape from last night looks a lot like you."

Frank felt his scalp tighten. Who'd have ever imagined a place like the Catacomb would have CCTV? Although, he didn't know why he was surprised. Seemed like you couldn't move a yard in London without appearing on some monitor or other.

"Plus, the tattooed angel on the front door remembers you, and could readily finger you."

All Frank could think was that he'd like to kill Donovan. Strangle him with his bare hands.

"All of which would indicate that you were within spitting distance of Kelly Anton … a huge celebrity. Now, I don't believe you can spit anywhere near the distance that the court order specified. What was it, Frank, something like not being less than a quarter of a mile away from any star or celebrity?"

Frank could easily wring Donovan's freckled neck until he turned blue and died.

"We need to talk," said Donovan. "Meet me at lunchtime.

12:30 at that pub around the corner from your office. Whassit called?"

"The Warwick," said Frank.

"That's the place," said Donovan and rang off.

Frank glowered at the phone in his hand for a few seconds before placing it back in the handset.

"Did I hear you taking my name in vain?" asked Ali.

Frank was inclined not to let Ali in on Donovan's discovery of their shenanigans.

"Like the Lord God you mean?" said Frank. "I got news for you Ali, despite your many talents, you're no deity."

He turned to his computer and opened a folder of pictures marked for uploading to one of the magazines the agency regularly supplied.

"Come on, spill it," said Ali, "Obviously something's gone down. Was that one of them sketchy photo editors?"

Frank supposed he owed it to the lad to explain. He gave him a quick rundown of Donovan's threats.

"Christ Frank, if your wanker of a son-in-law goes to the cops with the CCTV footage it could mean a stretch inside for you, am I right?"

"Thanks for the reminder," said Frank.

"We gotta get to him. Rash'll do it, he's heavy into Ju Jitsu, got belts and shit."

"And once he's given the chop to Donovan, then what? Rashid marries the tattooed girl to keep her sweet?"

"I don't think he'd go that far," said Ali.

Frank couldn't detect an iota of irony in Ali's comment. Normally he'd have considered teasing Ali by asking him why marrying the girl would be a bigger ask of Rashid than beating the shit out of Donovan. But the situation was too serious for any farting about.

"I've got a suspicion the bastard wants something, otherwise he'd have snitched on me already. Let me meet up with him and see what it is."

Frank left the office with time to spare, wanting to arrive at the Warwick before Donovan.

"You want me to come with?" asked Ali.

"That's very sweet of you," said Frank. "But I think I'll be okay on my own."

"Big mistake, but up to you," said Ali, showing no sign that he'd clued in to Frank's sarcasm.

The Warwick was a characterful old pub that, in Frank's opinion, had been ruined in misguided attempts to tart it up: recessed pot lights in the traditionally moulded ceiling, an exposed brick wall, and a couple of faux-Victorian ceiling fans. The place pitched itself as a 'gastropub.' Frank knew that its dubious conversion from quaint local to flashy eatery would doubtless be called 'rebranding' by the narrow-trouser-legged trendies who frequented the place. He suspected it was all a ruse to charge double what food used to cost, back in the days of a simple over-the-bar transaction.

He was asked by an unsmiling yet obsequious young man if he'd like a table. Frank was determined not to be intimidated by Donovan so he opted to sit at the bar, where his height and bulk would be more obvious, being right next to the little runt rather than across a table. He ordered a lemonade and, suspecting it would be the most expensive he'd ever drunk, he asked to run a tab. Donovan could pay for it,

Frank couldn't tell if it was the public location or the fact that Donovan must be aware that he was within punching range, but when his son-in-law showed up, he was a lot less threatening than he'd been on the phone. It was almost as though they were discussing an amicable business transaction.

"What I'm gonna need from you Frank, mate, is about a two-hour photo session with Kelly."

The pong of Donovan's aftershave was ruining the

taste of Frank's expensive lemonade. He remembered his daughter once mentioned it was Yves Saint Laurent 'Jazz,' and that Donovan liked it because of the name.

"First off, you're not my fucking mate," said Frank. "And second, if you think I'm going within a mile of Kelly Anton — a huge celebrity, as you put it earlier — you're badly mistaken."

Donovan smiled, took a sip of the pansy pink spritzer he'd ordered — Aperol, whatever the fuck that was. Frank had never heard of it.

"That ship has sailed, Frank," he said. "What would be the point of my getting you together with Kelly when I already have tape of you at the Catacomb."

Frank noticed there was none of Donovan's usual nervous nose-pulling. The bastard was obviously feeling cocky.

"What is your fucking point then?"

"I need some classy celebrity shots. And who better than you."

"I didn't think Kelly Anton was in any fit state."

"Don't you worry about that. She'll be well fit."

"What am I supposed to use for a camera? Not to mention lights? All my gear was sold off in the bankruptcy."

"I thought you sometimes used to rent equipment."

Frank cursed. How could the little prick have known. Maybe Whitney had mentioned it.

"Renting is beyond my means these days, I'm afraid."

"No worries, Frank. We're all kitted out at the office. I'll make sure to bring some top-notch tackle to match your high professional standards."

Donovan laced the last three words with sarcasm. Frank wondered what the tight-arsed manager would do if he laid Donovan out on the pub floor right there and then.

"If I do this, I want your promise — not that it's worth much — that the original CCTV recording has been wiped and your assurance that no copies were made."

"My word as a gentleman," said Donovan.

"As I said, not worth much."

Donovan shrugged, took another sip of his pink concoction.

"And you'll tell the tattooed princess to button it?"

"She don't even know what she saw. I just described you and she remembered. She don't know who you are, nor nothing about you. It's just that if I choose to fill her in, and ask her assistance …"

"Which you won't."

"Never. Well, not unless I have to."

Frank studied Donovan's freckled face, wondering what the hell was going through the little bastard's mind.

"You knew, didn't you?"

"What's that Frank, mate?"

"You knew when you told me on the bus about Kelly's gig that I'd find a way to nab some shots."

"Let's just say I suspected you'd bite."

"Why bother? You could just have used the camera in your new phone — I presume you can afford one — to knock off the shots of Kelly bottling it on stage that you needed for the gutter press. Why go to all this trouble just to involve me?"

"You could say I wanted it to be a family affair."

Frank grunted in disbelief. Ali had been correct in his over-the-phone assessment, Donovan was a freak. Frank had never understood what in the world his daughter, Whitney, saw in him. Maybe it was his family. Frank knew Whitney was bezzie mates with Donovan's sisters, who she'd once described as 'a hell of a laugh'. What does that make me? Frank had wondered.

One look at Donovan's family had been enough to confirm to Frank that Whitney was making a huge mistake, but by then the wedding was in progress. Protesting at that point was out of the question. He realized Whitney would never forgive him if he ruined her big day. Donovan's side of the church resembled a series of police line-ups rather than rows of pews at a marriage ceremony. With shaved heads, multiple piercings and little skin visible that didn't carry a tattoo, Donovan's male relatives looked to Frank like a gang of thugs and ASBOs. The females were a bunch of big-haired women with plunging necklines and exposed thighs. They were slathered with make-up that looked like it'd been applied with a spatula. Frank wouldn't have been surprised to learn that they were all on the game. Which may have been somewhat judgmental of him, but how was he supposed to know that, rather than being villains and tarts, the whole tribe was in the music industry?

The men were roadies, mostly. Except for a male cousin who'd had a one-hit wonder a few years back. And two of Donovan's sisters sang backup for anyone who'd have them. Eleanor Carter, Donovan's mother, was a different kettle of fish altogether. Her spindly arms and legs were at odds with her barrel-shaped mid-section. She had wispy dyed-red hair, white roots showing, and wore layers of floaty clothes that, were it not for her girth, might have given her an ethereal air. She told Frank wistfully that she'd been a folkie back in the day, played the lute and sang at country fairs and festivals. She was opening for Lindisfarne when she met Donovan's father. A mandolin player, she confided to Frank. She never saw him again after the tour was finished. Eleanor Carter had rubicund, puffy features as though sodden, subcutaneous clumps had gathered in inappropriate locations to form roseate mounds on her face and neck. It was a look that suggested an intimate relationship with booze and cigarettes — as Frank well knew. Nevertheless, Frank could imagine that Donovan's mother had probably been a looker as a young woman. Which made Frank wonder exactly how ugly his son-in-law's father must have been.

At the wedding party, in front of everyone, Donovan asked Frank if he could call him Dad.

"No fucking way," was Frank's knee-jerk reply.

He might have let his new son-in-law down a little more gently if he'd been sober. The one thing Frank remembered clearly was how Donovan couldn't have looked more hurt if Frank had hit him. And Frank had a vague recollection of all the other guests looking away in embarrassment. He'd certainly never forget the bollocking that Whitney gave him afterwards, drink befuddled though he was.

"Family means everything to him," she'd said over and again. "And he's never had a father."

But Frank had been unrepentant and unyielding.

"It'll be a cold day in hell when I ever call you Dad again then," she said.

And she'd kept her promise by refusing to have anything to do with Frank. Not answer to his calls, let alone a meet. Christ, but she'd been stubborn. In the end Frank had simply given up trying.

"When do you want to do this shoot?" Frank asked Donovan.

"Tomorrow night."

"Where?"

"Kelly's place. In her penthouse. I'll e-mail you the address."

"I haven't got personal e-mail and I don't want you using my FoodFoto address, so think again." The truth was Frank couldn't afford an internet connection, but he wasn't going to tell his cocky son-in-law.

Donovan pulled out one of his yellow business cards and wrote on the back.

"This is her building. I'll meet you outside at seven."

He thrust the piece of paper into Frank's hand.

"Now let's 'ave a bite and catch up, whaddya say Frank? Just like old times."

Donovan really was delusional. As far as Frank could remember they'd never had a meal together, not just the two of them. He was buggered if he wasn't going to start now. He slid off the bar stool and stood just long enough to say, "See you tomorrow, around 7:00. Alright?"

As he walked away, he heard Donovan say, "Don't be like that, Frank."

"Thanks for the lemonade," he shouted back.

By the time Frank arrived back at FoodFoto he was weak with hunger. He couldn't wait to get his hands on the lunch he'd brought from home. Whacking great ham and cheese sandwich. Which, when waved in front of Ali, would be good for a few ripe comments from the vegetarian Muslim, although he couldn't very well disapprove of the whole-grain bread, having gone on about its health-giving ingredients.

"Frank, thank Christ! You'd best get downstairs and comfort your boyfriend," said Cheryl, the receptionist, as soon as he stepped in the front door of the agency. "There's been a mad Jamaican here, screaming threats at him."

"What? Where?" said Frank.

"Here. Just now," said Cheryl. "Ali came up and calmed him down a bit, but he was still effing and blinding. He scarpered when I said I was calling the police. The boss is none too happy about the kerfuffle."

Frank almost fell down the narrow stairs to the basement in his hurry to talk to Ali. The lad was sitting at his computer, but staring, hands motionless, at a photo of an ice cream sundae on the screen.

"You alright, Ali? What the hell happened?"

Ali turned to look at Frank. His face, normally a full-bodied coffee colour, appeared more like milky Nescafé.

"He threatened to beat the shit out of me, Frank. In't no-one ever done that before."

"Why? Who the hell is he?"

"Only Kelly Anton's father, innit."

After much probing and pushing it emerged that the man who'd claimed he was Kelly Anton's father had seen some of the photos from the Catacomb that they'd sold and was raging about them, particularly the one of her stumbling off stage.

"How in God's name did he know they were anything to do with you?" asked Frank.

Ali turned back to the computer and muttered something so low Frank didn't catch it.

"What?"

Ali turned back toward Frank, but kept his eyes lowered.

"There was one place last night what asked about running a credit with the photo. I didn't see the harm."

"Shit, Ali. Which publication was it?"

"The Voice. Who ever heard of it?"

"It's only the biggest African-Caribbean newspaper in Britain," said Frank. "No wonder Kelly's old man is upset. It'll be the paper him and all his mates read."

"How was I to know?"

Frank stared at Ali, who still gazed at the floor, and thought about how the lust for recognition passed nobody by. Ali had given in to the temptation of a fraction of fame, even if it was his name in impossibly small type running up the side of a photo. Frank could hardly criticize — he'd been there more than once.

"But I thought 'Khawaja' was like the 'Smith' of Pakistan. Millions of you, aren't there?"

"We're not that common," said Ali in an injured tone despite his sheepishness.

"So how the fuck did he find you?"

"Linkedin," said Ali.

"Linked-sodding-in!"

"I know, it's lame. But anything to get me out of this bloody cellar, innit. My profile's got the photography course

I done, and that I work at FoodFoto, and other photography stuff. Mr Anton — if that's who he really is — must have stumbled on it through Google or some other search engine, put two and two together, and got lucky."

Ali smiled ruefully.

Frank shook his head. He couldn't help smiling. Linkedin, for fuck's sake.

"Cheryl said you talked to him."

Ali described how he'd heard a man shouting his name, so he went upstairs to see what all the fuss was about. By that time Bertie Big Bollocks was retreating into his office.

"He just closes his door, the bastard. Leaves me and Cheryl to deal with a murderous mad man," said Ali.

Ali told Frank how, after he'd calmed the Jamaican down a bit, the man had written his address and phone number on one of Cheryl's post-its and said he wanted a proper written apology, or else.

"And you won't fucking believe this, Frank. He says he wants me to say sorry to his daughter too, face to face like."

Ali's complexion had almost returned to its normal wholesome colour and his eyes shone.

"If he really is Kelly Anton's father, I'll be meeting her … in person."

"I'd have thought you'd have had enough of her."

"You're joking. I in't even started," said Ali.

JASON DOZED FOR the rest of the morning. Kelly assumed he was still suffering the effects of the Rohypnol. He hadn't asked again about his crack-in-a-box. She wondered if he was holding off to prove — to her? to himself? — that he wasn't hooked.

Jason had always said that a lot of what the press wrote

about crack was rubbish. They claimed all it took was one puff to make you a raging addict, immediately prone to mugging your own mother for money to buy more.

"It's all media bullshit," Jason had said. "There are loads of white-collar crack users — city boys who work like stink all week, pulling in thousands. Then they get their jollies at the weekend with a few pipes. No harm done."

Kelly knew that even a casual user would need to be earning a bundle. She'd occasionally been with Jason when he shelled out for a few rocks, and was well aware that, at twenty quid or more for a small piece, just smoking enough to stay chilled for a weekend would cost a chunk of change. Jason couldn't have afforded it on only the wages he earned as a "lackey," as he called the part-time job he had, more because he went to school with the production company owner than because of his MBA. Which, according to Jason, "they give to every wanker with half a brain and enough money to pay the fee." However, Jason was 'allowed' a thousand or more a month from a family trust fund — pocket money, as he called it — that helped pay for his occasional high.

Around two o'clock Kelly decided she was peckish for some Italian nosh. She may not have been able to go to a restaurant without being harassed by fans between every mouthful, but she could always order in. Although she sometimes missed not being able to drop into anywhere she fancied at the drop of a hat, Kelly only had to call almost any restaurant in London and say who she was, give them her VISA number, and they'd put something together for her and send it off in a cab. One of the perks of fame.

Since she was a kid, Kelly had known an Italian family that owned a restaurant on Battersea High Street, she'd gone to primary school with one of the daughters. Before her 'big break,' as Jason laughingly called it, she'd often eaten there. Since she'd moved into the penthouse just up the road, they'd made her whatever she wanted and delivered it to her.

"Wake up, Jase," she said. "I'm ordering from Primavera, you want anything?"

He asked for eggplant parmigiana.

"And ask them to throw in a can or two of that fizzy drink."

"Chinotto," said Kelly.

"That's the stuff. And a big dollop of tiramisu."

"Someone's hungry," said Kelly.

"I'm bloody ravenous. You'd think for the money they charge at that hospital they'd give you a better breakfast."

Kelly didn't own a dining table. She and Jason always ate, usually right out of containers that the food came in, sprawled out on the bed. It didn't do much for the state of the sheets, but Kelly liked the casual feel of it. Plus, it kept washing-up to a minimum. Kelly could only count on one hand the number of times they'd used the fancy Miele dishwasher that came with the penthouse.

"That was bloody delicious," said Jason, plopping an empty container onto the floor beside the bed.

Kelly was still working on her food. Hungry as she thought she'd been, she was having trouble swallowing. She put the polystyrene plate to one side, half of her fettucine alfredo uneaten. Deep breath. It was now or never.

"You know you always claim that the media don't know what the fuck they're talking about?" she asked.

"You of all people know how true it is," said Jason.

"I'm not arguing," said Kelly, but then she faltered.

"What then?" asked Jason, after a few seconds of silence.

"Don't freak out, okay."

"Whenever anybody says that, it means there's something worth freaking out about. What is it?"

Kelly could feel her heart speed up, almost as bad as

before going on stage. She worried she might lose what little pasta she'd eaten.

"You know all these stories the last few weeks about me — us — being high and out of control and shit?"

"Yes, what about them?" asked Jason.

"They might have come from Donovan ..."

"Is the man fucking insane or what?"

"... and me," said Kelly, her voice quavering.

Jason looked at her, eyes narrowed.

"You?"

Then it all came pouring out. Kelly babbled on about her not being able to come up with lyrics, how worried she'd been about producing a second album, and how Donovan had come up with the scheme about making out she was drug addled to keep her in the news until she could come up with new material. She told Jason about her going along with it all.

"You've been calling the press to tell them you're out of your head?"

"Sometimes, yes."

"And they swallowed it?"

"Hook, line, and everything else."

Jason whistled.

"Wow," he said. "How could they be so stupid? You didn't really look bad. Maybe a bit knackered, and sometimes I wondered about the clothes. But I thought it was just you playing the anti-celebrity."

Kelly was relieved he seemed to be taking the news so well. He even seemed impressed.

"It was easy peasy. I'd just plant the idea in their heads that they was gagging to hear — Kelly Anton out of her tree in public — and Bingo! There they were. Like, whassit called? Carrion around a dead deer."

"Carrion actually is the dead deer. I think the word you're looking for is scavengers."

129

Jason wasn't one to condescend, and Kelly could detect a hostile edge in his voice. Was he more pissed off than he appeared?

"I'm really sorry, Jase. I never thought you'd get so smeared by the bastards as well. It was just I was at my wit's end, and you know how Donovan puts on the pressure."

Jason stood up. After the scorching lecture he delivered from the end of the bed, Kelly was wishing to hell he had freaked out. Instead, he logically and completely destroyed her, point by point. He never raised his voice. He didn't once resort to swear words or bad language. He merely expressed every single thought she'd had herself about how selfish, stupid, and harmful the plan had been — and a few more besides. By the end of it, Kelly had never felt so trashed.

"Not to mention the fact that you let — actually facilitated — me to become the object of scurrilous reports and accusations that were completely untrue," Jason concluded.

Kelly, in total panic mode about losing him, but also desperate to defend herself any way she could, even if she knew deep down that her actions were indefensible, thought about pointing out to Jason that he did actually use drugs. He may not be a raving addict, like the papers described him, but he had, after all, been high in some of the photos. But before she had a chance, he delivered the final thrust that left her struggling to breathe.

"The ridiculous thing is that I was beginning to think you were the one. That I'd fallen in love, at last."

He grabbed some clothes and stuffed them into a bag.

"Wait Jason, there's more," said Kelly, having decided to spill it all. What difference did it make now if he knew everything?

"I don't want to hear it Kelly. I'll send somebody to pick up my chairs."

And he was gone.

THE PAPARAZZO AND THE POP STAR

"I WISH RASH WAS here," said Ali.

"What's Rashid got that I haven't?" asked Frank.

"Only a black belt in Ju Jitsu."

"He's never been sent down for A.B.H. though, has he?"

Ali was quick to point out that Frank hadn't exactly been 'sent down'.

"Only a suspended sentence, wasn't it?"

"It's still a bloody conviction," said Frank, not quite believing he was using his violent crime as some sort of qualification. A duff-up diploma, or a certificate for random acts of violence.

"It'd be better if it'd been that other thing … Grievous Bodily Harm," said Ali.

When Ali had told Frank that Rashid was working and couldn't go with him to deliver his letter of apology to Kelly Anton's father, Frank had insisted on accompanying the lad.

"Oh, so I'm not allowed to come with you to protect you from Mr. Big Shot Record Producer, but it's fine for you to come with me to see Kelly Anton's murderous Dad?"

"Do you want me to come, or not?" asked Frank.

When Frank saw Ali's apology letter, he couldn't believe it was a computer print-out.

"Don't you think you should write it by hand?"

"Why? I'm gonna sign it, innit."

On second thoughts it was probably better that way, thought Frank, remembering how illegible Ali's handwriting was. Mind you, his own wasn't too hot either, he was so out of practice. Frank wondered if there'd be a time not far off when no-one could actually write, just tap away at a keyboard.

"I don't know why you're delivering it by hand, anyway. It's just asking for trouble."

"He said it had to be in person, and today. By six o'clock, or else. Whatever that meant."

The road they were looking for was supposed to be the first one they reached after the bus dropped them at Latchmere Leisure Centre.

"Here we are," said Ali. "Matthews Street."

"What number?"

"Eight," said Ali.

The two-storey terraced houses seemed toy-like to Frank. He may only inhabit one room, but it was wider than one of these houses. The building he lived in was run-down, but it was a four-storey, porticoed Georgian that once would have been considered grand.

At least the even-numbered side of Matthews Street consisted of single-family houses. Frank could see by the double front doors on the odd-numbered side that each house was split into two flats, one up, one down. Swinging a cat would definitely not be an option in any of the units on that side of the street. Despite the scale, Frank could tell by smart wooden-louvered shutters and brightly painted front doors with gleaming steel or brass hardware that many, if not most, of the street's residents were anything but working class. Frank wondered if Kelly Anton had bought her father's house for him.

White liberal guilt seeped in when Frank immediately realized he'd assumed a Jamaican couldn't afford to buy in such a gentrified London neighbourhood. He felt somewhat justified in his assumption when he saw an original paint-encrusted door knocker and simple net curtains on the front windows of number eight. It was obvious that Mr. Anton had in all likelihood lived there since before the street was invaded by middle-class 'yummy mummies' and their families, with a resulting rise in property value. The Anton front door was as freshly painted as the others, but in a lurid turquoise gloss that screamed

'Caribbean' — to Frank, at least. One thing for sure, it wasn't ultra-chic Farrow and Ball, which he was willing to bet was the brand of paint used on other front doors up and down the street.

"You ready?" asked Frank.

Ali muttered something in Urdu, by the sound of it. A prayer, Frank assumed. Then he nodded.

Frank knocked on the door.

After a long pause he was about to knock again when there was a clattering noise on the other side of the door.

"Raas claat. Ruth! Why you no leave yuh bike out the back?"

"Me soon come," the voice shouted, over what Frank took to be metal mudguards clattering.

The door was thrust open. A wiry man, around Frank's age and height, but skinnier, peered at them. He sported a shock of white curls on top of his head, the sides shaved almost to the scalp.

"I brung the letter like you asked, innit," said Ali.

Frank could hear the nervousness in Ali's abrupt manner. It was clear he was flustered.

The man transferred his gaze to Frank. He frowned. Seconds ticked by and the man said nothing. He stared intently at Frank.

Just as Frank was about to say something, the man said, "Frank? Frank McCann?"

Frank was too transfixed by the man's recognition of him to look at Ali, but he could sense the lad's astonishment. Frank returned the man's gaze. The white-haired man looked vaguely familiar, but from where? Frank struggled to remember how the hell he might know him. Had he once snapped him? Oh, God, please don't let Kelly Anton's father be somebody he'd photographed against his will. But the man seemed genuinely delighted. He beamed, teeth impossibly white, eyes shining.

"Frank, man. It you innit?"

"Yes," said Frank, "Yes, it's me."

"Rhaatid! Ruth, Ruth! Come see who the cat drag in."

A woman appeared in the hall. She held a mobile phone up to her ear.

"Gotta go, love. There's someone at the door," she said.

As she approached, Frank could see that she too had white hair, but in contrast to the man's it fell, completely straight, and was cut severely in a line just below her ears. Enquiring blue eyes, framed by deep laugh lines, inspected Frank. She prompted a memory that flickered on the edge of Frank's consciousness, only just out of reach, like a name on the tip of his tongue. He scowled with the effort of straining to recall. When the woman reached the front door, the man turned to her.

"It Frank McCann, from Wolverhampton, you mind?"

Wolverhampton! Like a lock combination falling into place, the pieces all flew together. Wolverhampton, where Frank had been at art college. Frank's fake photograph from back then, with its unthinkable result. The horrific few days following, when he and Christine were trying to prove a man's innocence. This man. His building-site pal. And the woman standing behind him, the lawyer whom Frank had heard his Jamaican friend had married.

"Nelson?"

Frank knew it to be him but couldn't make sense of it. What were Nelson — Nelson Clarke — and Ruth doing in Kelly Anton's father's house?

Suddenly all three of them were talking at once.

"Wha' the hell you doing here wi' this ginnal bwoy?" demanded Nelson.

"What are you doing in this house?" asked Frank.

"How's Christine? Where are you living?" said Ruth.

Then all three stopped abruptly. They looked at each other for a second, then fell about laughing. Nelson, in particular, hooted and chortled long after Frank and Ruth had stopped. When Frank stole a look at Ali, he could see that the lad must have been thinking he'd arrived at a lunatic asylum.

There followed a short explanation on the doorstep from Frank about how he and Ali worked together. That he could explain everything about the shots of Kelly in The Voice. Nelson appeared dubious. He looked at Ali suspiciously.

"Frank man, it feel like maybe we back in Wolverhampton dealin' with photo trickery."

"I know, I know," said Frank. "But it's not so bad, I promise."

Then it occurred to him that he was being put on the defensive.

"Why did you pretend to be Kelly Anton's father?"

Nelson's eyes grew wide. He was clearly indignant.

"No pretendin' Frank. I is her true father."

Frank must have appeared perplexed, because Ruth stepped in to explain.

"You're thinking about the name. Kelly changed hers to Anton when she started performing. She thought Kelly Clarke sounded too much like a country singer."

Frank could see the logic in that. Kelly Clarke did have a Nashville ring to it.

"Anton is my grandfather's name, my mother's father," said Ruth. "The story is that we're descended from Huguenots."

The realization that he'd banged into Ruth and Nelson in such a serendipitous fashion was too much for Frank. He took a deep breath and blew it out, shaking his head and raising his eyebrows in disbelief.

"But we want to hear all about you. Come in, come in," insisted Ruth. She took him by the arm and pulled him over the threshold and into the hall.

135

"You too," said Nelson, when Ali hung back. "Any friend o' Frank, no matter what you done."

There followed a half-hour of reminiscing among the three older people over cups of tea. Ali never said a word, he just looked from one to the other as each spoke.

"I keep a copy of that paper, you know," said Nelson. "It upstair somewhere."

"Never mind about that," called Ruth after his retreating figure. "You'll be late for your gig."

"I no say?" shouted Nelson. "They call this mornin' to cancel."

While he was upstairs looking for the old student newspaper, Frank felt the need to explain to Ali. But his workmate seemed to have followed the gist of their conversation.

"So, you faked a photo when you was at art school," said Ali. "You put ... Mr. Whassisname ..."

"Clarke," said Ruth.

"... into a place he never was," continued Ali. " So it ruined his alibi, which was true, and put him at the scene and time of a murder, when he wasn't really there at all."

"Well, you make it sound worse than it was," said Frank. "I didn't implicate him on purpose."

Frank was at a loss. How could he explain to Ali that he'd had no idea when he superimposed Nelson into the photo of a student demonstration in Wolverhampton it would land Nelson in so much trouble.

"Actually, Ali," said Ruth. "Nelson was a lot angrier about your photo in The Voice than he ever was about Frank's faked shot."

Ali had the good grace to look less judgmental.

"It's not about you really." She reached out and laid her hand reassuringly on Ali's arm. "He's so upset about Kelly in general, it just set him off."

Before she could elaborate, Nelson appeared, triumphantly waving the copy of VoxPop, the student newspaper.

THE PAPARAZZO AND THE POP STAR

Frank couldn't believe he'd held on to it for forty years.

"I notice there's a credit on the photo," said Ali, looking meaningfully at Frank. "Oh look, it says 'Frank McCann.'"

"You're not the only one who's been so thirsty for fame and recognition that he didn't consider the consequences," said Frank.

"And you say you did this old-school style? Cutting up prints and that?" asked Ali, examining the photo closely.

"Of course," said Frank. "No computers and no Photoshop in those days."

"It's bloody good," said Ali.

"Too bloody good," said Nelson.

Even after all that had happened and the years that had passed, Frank felt a glow of self-satisfaction. He felt particularly chuffed to have Ali's approval.

Ruth stood to clear away the tea things. Frank was just about to suggest they take off, when there was the sound of the front door opening. There was a clang and a metallic clatter. The door had obviously hit the bicycle.

"Christ, Mum," said a woman's voice. "Why do you always leave your bike in the bloody hall?"

Frank noticed Nelson's face change. His jaw clenched. Muscles stood out on either side of his face. His eyes, until then a soft velveteen brown, seemed to darken.

"Kelly, love. We're back here," shouted Ruth.

Frank glanced at Ali. He'd never seen the lad's eyes open so wide.

"Is dad there?" Kelly had asked her mother. Jason had been gone more than an hour and she thought if she didn't talk to someone, she might throw herself off the terrace, or go barking mad.

"Yes, but not for long," said Ruth. "I told you he had a gig later."

"If I walk over now, will he be gone by the time I get there?"

"Should be. But if you're walking, watch out for stalkers."

Normally Kelly would have given her mother shit for putting the wind up her. As far as she knew, there were no weirdos following her, but you never knew. However, at that moment all she could think about was getting out of the penthouse, where Jason so obviously wasn't.

"Gotta go, love," said her mother. "There's someone at the door."

Kelly told herself if she didn't dawdle and did the disguise thing, with dark glasses and a head scarf, like when she'd gone to the Catacomb, she should go unnoticed. She could walk mostly through the park. There'd be few people there at that time on a weekday, and once out the other side she could take the quieter side-streets to Matthews Street. Maybe the walk would clear her head. It might even take her mind of Jason. Sod him. Whenever she began to feel guilty all over again about not telling Jason about her subterfuge, she'd told herself that he was no fucking angel either. But it didn't help the overwhelming feeling of desolation that had put her on the edge or panic since he'd left.

With the sun on her face and a refreshing breeze blowing, Kelly felt better. She was glad she'd decided not to take a cab. The air in the penthouse that day had felt particularly stale. So much for all the hype about fancy air filters and cutting-edge heating and cooling systems. And if she opened the terrace doors, Jason always complained about drafts, saying he'd had enough for a lifetime, as a child living in the big old piles his family owned. She supposed she could have the frigging doors open 24/7 now that Jason had gone. But she'd have happily put up with stale air — even welcomed the occasional chemical stench of burning crack — if he came back. But somehow, she didn't think that was likely, given how injured he'd seemed.

Once out of the park she had to take Albert Bridge Road, but the few people she passed seemed to take no notice of her. It wasn't long before she was able to deke over to the Latchmere Recreation Ground, she breathed easier, being back on her home turf. She could see the bushes over in the corner where she and her friend, Sharon, lit up a cigarette for the first time. Kelly never really took to it, but Sharon puffed away with the best of them. Kelly snogged her first proper boyfriend, Lee Jacobs, over there too. With his hand down her cut-off jeans, Lee had given her her first — and astounding — orgasm one warm summer evening.

She supposed from the outside it might look like she inhabited two different worlds, going from a vast riverside penthouse to the tiny terraced house where she'd grown up and where her parents still lived, but it didn't feel like that to Kelly. As far as she was concerned, she never wanted to be a super star. She was just always trying to be a better musician — and she was still trying. That hadn't ever changed, it was always what it was all about. Nothing else mattered, except maybe Jason. So, the two locations — posh residence and childhood home — didn't seem all that different to her.

Even so, in the last few years, whenever Kelly turned into Matthews Street, she was struck by its transformation. The houses were the same houses, of course, but in less than a decade the place had gone from a raucous working-class block to a silent yuppy enclave. When she was growing up, there'd rarely been a moment when you didn't hear the sound of kids yelling or mothers screaming their names to come in for their tea. Now the only time you ever saw kids was when they were hustled between car and front door by overly protective parents. And that was another thing that had changed — when Kelly was little there were almost no parked cars. Now the street was lined end to end with Audis, BMWs, and other high-end motors. Her parents and old Mrs Saunders at number twelve were the only people who'd lived there longer than fifteen years.

Kelly could never quite analyze the not unpleasant smell of her parent's hallway, unique as it was to their house. Freshly painted walls or newly laid carpet had occasionally banished the distinctive smell, but it slowly seeped back again. Which Kelly always found irrationally reassuring. Although she was regularly irritated by her mother's habit of leaving her old bike just where the front door would hit it, Kelly was always comforted by the familiar aroma that greeted her once she was inside.

Her mother's voice called from the kitchen. What did she mean by "We're back here?" Her Dad was supposed to be out. But she couldn't very well turn tail now, and maybe it was somebody else. Kelly walked warily down the narrow hall. She was amazed to be confronted by four people huddled round the kitchen table. One of them being her father, for Christ's sake.

"Bloody hell, Kelly, what do you look like?" her mother said.

Kelly had forgotten about the dark glasses. She whipped them off and glared at her mother.

"Is that supposed to be a disguise? You might as well hold up a sign," said her mother, laughing. "'Famous person here, trying not to look like it.'"

"What are you on about?"

"Only the Queen and women who think it'll make them invisible go about in a headscarf and sunglasses."

"It true, Kelly love. It mek you stick out like a sore thumb," said her father.

If the two strangers hadn't been there, Kelly would have

told him she didn't need him putting his oar in, but as it was, she kept shtum.

"I like it," said one of the two others, an older man with a shock of grayish dirty blonde hair. "Very retro. Reminds me of Audrey Hepburn — not that I ever met her."

Bit of a weird thing to say — about never meeting somebody as big as Audrey Hepburn — thought Kelly. Who the hell was this bloke?

"This gentleman is an old friend of your father," said her mother.

The man stood. He was fit for his age, which Kelly assumed was the same as her father's. His face was lined and a bit gaunt, but the wear and tear probably saved him from looking ordinary.

"Frank McCann," said the man. "Really good to meet you."

"And this…" said her father, gesturing toward the younger man, who had that rabbit-in-the-headlights look people often had when they first met her, "… is the bad bwoy what took the photo of you in that club, where you lookin' so wreck."

Trust her Dad to put the cat among the pigeons. Kelly couldn't believe the ruckus that ensued. The 'bwoy' just kept saying sorry over and again, but at the same time he was giving the evil eye to her father. Her Mum was giving her father shit about it being "downright unfair" to introduce the "poor lad" like that. The man, Frank, was insisting it was all his fault. Then, when her father realized she wasn't impressed by him having found the kid who'd snapped the photos, he lost it and accused her of "bein' so drug up she forget 'ow to say t'ankyou." They were all gesticulating and talking over each other.

Kelly snapped. She yelled at the top of her voice, so loud, thanks to the breathing lessons she'd had, she could probably be heard in every house up and down the street.

"Shut the fuck up, all of you."

They all stared at her silently, except for her father, who still muttered something about "that junkie Jason" being to blame. Kelly let out a growl of frustration and stormed out of the house.

When her mother caught up with her, she insisted they walk together back through the park to Kelly's building.

"And take that stupid headscarf off, you look like some rich bitch."

"I am a rich bitch," said Kelly.

Her mother's expression of exaggerated shock was priceless. Kelly couldn't help smiling. She remembered occasions when her mother had always found a way to lighten the mood. Whether Kelly had been upset by a scraped knee or hadn't had a good mark from her music teacher, or, once or twice, had been dumped by a boy. Her mother always managed to buck up her spirits.

"Anyway, I thought working women used to wear scarves like this too," she said, folding it up and putting it in her coat pocket.

"Yeah, but not Gucci, or Pucci, or whatever expensive silk number that one obviously is," said Ruth.

"Versace, actually," said Kelly, in an exaggeratedly posh voice.

She took her mother's arm in hers and pulled it affectionately to her body.

The lightened mood seemed to give her mother the opportunity to bring up Kelly's father again.

"He's only doing what he thinks is right, for your sake, love," she said.

"That might be, but what he has to realize is, the longer this goes on the deeper in the shit I sink."

"Do you have to put it quite like that?" asked Ruth.

"And I miss him."

"I'm sure you do," said Ruth. "But is it for the right reasons?"

"No, Mum. I swear, I miss our times messing around at the piano, no matter what came out of them."

Kelly stared ahead at the path meandering through the park. What could she say? They'd been over the same ground again and again.

A young couple, who'd been walking toward them, stopped suddenly more or less right in front of them. The woman was fishing in her handbag. Kelly knew what was coming.

"I hope you don't mind," said the girl breathlessly. The bloke looked mildly embarrassed, but stared at Kelly, nevertheless.

Kelly took the ballpoint and what appeared to be a supermarket receipt and scribbled her name on the back. She handed it back with a tight smile. What the fuck did people do with their little scraps of paper, she wondered. At least they weren't asking for that selfie thing that every fan had begun to demand.

"Thank you very much. We love your music."

Kelly nodded, smiled again a little more warmly, and took her mother's arm again, which prompted the couple to move aside. Kelly was about to tell her mother — as a joke — that she should have kept her headscarf on, but Ruth carried on with the conversation as though nothing out of the ordinary had happened.

"I know your Dad's asked you to dump Jason, but I don't think you have to go that far. You just need to prove to him somehow that you've cleaned up your act. Both of you."

Kelly's heart sunk.

"You haven't heard about last night's drama, have you?" she asked.

"What drama?"

"You're gonna hear them saying that Jason overdosed, but he didn't. I swear. He was drugged, yes. But someone spiked his coffee."

"Jesus, Kelly. Your Dad's upset as it is. This'll send him over the edge."

"Just tell him Jason and me have split up."

"I'm not lying for you, Kelly."

Kelly explained it was no lie, that Jason had walked out on her. She made out it was because he couldn't take being in the press all the time, but then was appalled when her mother took it the wrong way.

"The snotty bastard. Just 'cos he gets a bit of bad press. He knew what he was taking on when he shacked up with you."

"It's not that simple," said Kelly.

Ruth didn't ask. Kelly assumed she thought it was just a normal couple thing. How could she know about lying to the press?

"At least now maybe you can clean up your act. You will, won't you love?"

Kelly was consumed with guilt to think she couldn't relieve her mother's obvious concern by telling her she'd never touched anything stronger than a barley wine in years. She could try insisting again, but what was the point? Her mother wouldn't believe her, not after all the media shite. Kelly needed to prove it. She could only do it by telling her mother about Donovan's scheme, and she couldn't bring herself to do that. Especially after the effect it had had on Jason. She doubted that Ruth would believe it anyway.

"Honest to God, Mum, no more of my shenanigans in the press, I promise," Kelly said, emphatically. "Or out of the press, come to that."

At least she could keep her promise. No matter what Donovan thought or how he took it, she was determined to give up the stupid druggie act.

"Tell me who that geezer in your kitchen was, who seemed worried that I might think he'd really known Audrey Hepburn?"

Her mother said the bloke in the kitchen was Nelson's old mate from years ago, when they were all living in Wolverhampton. She said that she and Nelson had hung out with Frank and his girlfriend, Christine for a while. Frank moved to London to be a photographer. They'd lost touch after that.

"He told us he'd once been one of those photographers that take pictures of celebrities. Maybe that's why he made that Audrey Hepburn comment."

"Jesus, a bloody pap," said Kelly. "How did he end up in your house today? And how did that kid manage to take photos of me?"

"I don't know what you mean. All I know is that Frank works with Ali and he came along to make sure your father didn't kill the poor lad. Frank had no idea Nelson was your dad. It was pure coincidence that they'd been friends years ago."

"Somehow he don't seem like he'd be a pal of Dad's."

"They once worked together on a building site. And then Frank doctored a photo that got your father into a bit of trouble," said Ruth. "It's a long story."

"We've got all day," said Kelly. "Come up and tell me all about it. I can't stand the thought of rattling around that bleeding penthouse on my own."

"I CAN'T WAIT TO tell Rash that Kelly Anton called me 'that creepy little twat with the big glasses,'" said Ali.

Frank turned his attention from staring down the road, willing their bus to arrive. He frowned and looked at his young workmate.

145

"Let me get this straight," said Frank. "You're all in a huff when her Dad calls you a 'bad bwoy,' but when Kelly Anton abuses you it's cause for celebration?"

"Mr Anton, or Mr Clarke, whatever his name is, is a nobody, innit. But her … she's a megastar. And Rash will be well pleased that Kelly Anton's got his glasses on her radar."

Frank shook his head. He'd have thought that seeing Kelly in her parents' modest house having a melt down like any other spoilt brat, might have taken away some of the awe with which the star-struck Ali regarded her. But obviously not. Kelly Anton could shit all over the lad and he'd not only thank her but ask if he could please wipe her backside too.

Frank didn't blame Nelson for trying to use Ali to get back into Kelly's good books. It was obvious that Nelson hoped Ali's apology for taking and selling the photos, and the opportunity he was giving Kelly to give the lad what-for, would help settle their differences. It had been excruciating to listen to Nelson cajoling Kelly, telling her all the trouble he'd had to locate Ali. But it had all gone pear-shaped when Nelson became exasperated at his daughter's lack of gratitude. Frank guessed from something Ruth had said that there'd been some history of Nelson quarrelling with Kelly about her crackhead boyfriend. Frank knew from experience that a daughter can break a father's heart with her choice of a lover, or — worse — a husband. He recalled reports of Kelly and the boyfriend being out of their heads in public, clubs and the like. Or maybe Ali had mentioned it. Whatever, when Nelson started badmouthing the boyfriend, Kelly had lost it completely and stormed out, with her mother in hot pursuit. But not before Kelly had hurled a few insults at them all, including the one that so delighted Ali.

After Ruth had taken off after Kelly, Nelson thundered

on about how ungrateful Kelly was. He swore he didn't know why he'd helped her in the past. All the hours he'd put in with her at the "raas claat piano," as he put it. Frank presumed Nelson was talking about teaching her music as a child. The things parents dredged up to wave in front of their kids. Frank's daughter, Whitney, used to yell, "who asked you?" if he held up anything that he'd done for her. And Frank had to admit she sometimes wasn't wrong to ask the question.

Once Frank and Ali were installed in seats upstairs on the bus, Ali, who was still buzzing with excitement, said, "I know they talk about everybody being only six degrees of separation away from everybody else, like in that film, but what are the chances of you knowing Kelly Anton's father?"

Frank didn't respond. He felt dazed, finding it hard to believe the events of the last couple of hours had really happened.

"Does that make you two degrees from Kelly Anton, or just the one?" asked Ali.

"I don't fucking know," said Frank. "And I don't much care."

But then, as he gazed out at the lights of shops along Battersea Park Road, the thought came to him that it made sense that the longer you lived and the more people you encountered, the fewer the so-called 'degrees of separation' might become. He wasn't sure how he felt about it all, although he was genuinely pleased to be back in touch with his old friend, Nelson.

The next morning Frank made sure he arrived at the office early. If there were negotiations to be made with Donovan, he'd prefer Ali wasn't around to overhear them. Frank had been awake most of the night, worrying about what Kelly's reaction might be when he turned up to shoot whatever photos Donovan was insisting that he take of her that evening. Kelly was bound to get the wrong idea the minute she saw Frank, a man who'd been introduced to her as "an old friend of your father's." Chances were, she'd think Nelson was somehow involved with whatever it was that Donovan was up to. The last thing Frank wanted was to make life more difficult for Nelson. Frank doubted his son-in-law knew what a better nature was, let alone owned one, but he thought he'd appeal to it anyway. He didn't want Donovan to know about his connection to Nelson, so all he could do was beg. As it turned out, he shouldn't have wasted his time.

"Up to you, mate," said Donovan, when Frank phoned him. "Turn up tonight, or not."

His fake nonchalance really got up Frank's nose.

"But remember, if you decide not to show up, the courts don't look too kindly on someone breaking the conditions of their suspended sentence. 'Specially when they've been so fucking lenient in the first place."

Whether it was lack of sleep, or the daily grind of his own existence — or both — Frank didn't know. All he knew was that he lost it. His eyes seemed to fill with scarlet as his blood pressure skyrocketed. He must have ranted for a good thirty seconds. After he ran out of steam, he knew it was a mistake to show Donovan how much the little wanker had got to him. He was annoyed but not surprised when he heard Donovan on the other end of the phone say, "See you later then, mate." As jauntily as if he'd persuaded Frank to do nothing more momentous than meet him down the pub for an amiable after-work pint. Frank slammed the phone down.

"Someone sounds stressed," said Ali with exaggerated sibilance. He was standing in the doorway, his black leather man-bag dangling from one shoulder. He looked inquiringly at Frank with arched eyebrows.

"Come on then, spill," he said, with wide-eyed emphasis on the word 'spill.'

Frank couldn't help himself. He smiled, although weakly.

"For fuck's sake, Ali, what are you like?"

Ali pursed his lips and raised his eyebrows, continuing the camp act, whether consciously or not, Frank couldn't tell. Ali marched over to his desk, took off his coat and hung it and his man bag on the back of his chair.

"Well, are you going to tell me or not?" he said.

Frank didn't debate for long. Didn't they say that a problem shared was a problem halved? And he still liked Ali, even if he found the lad's irrational idolization of Kelly Anton disappointing. Not that he was unfamiliar with it. When he'd been a paparazzo, it was people like Ali who had made him a bundle. All those millions who'd bought magazines and newspapers featuring his photos of the rich and famous.

Frank told Ali how Donovan was leaning on him to take photos of Kelly. He didn't use the word 'blackmail,' but Ali got the picture right off the bat.

"Bloody hell, Frank. With Kelly's Dad scaring the shit out of me, I totally forgot to ask how the lunch with your psycho son-in-law went. I can see why you'd be so bent out of shape. Isn't there nothing you can do?"

"I've got no option but to go along with it and hope the bastard doesn't shop me anyway. But I'm worried how Kelly will react when she sees me."

Ali looked thoughtful.

"Well if you think of anything me and Rash could do, don't hesitate, alright?"

"Thanks, Ali," said Frank.

They both started into work. But after about five minutes Ali turned to look at Frank.

"Whatever you done to that son-in-law of yours must have been fucking major, innit."

149

He was clearly not expecting an answer and Frank didn't attempt one. But Ali's comment gave him pause. He thought about Nelson's vehemence when he was dissing Kelly's boyfriend. Had he been as insensitive about Donovan to Whitney as Nelson appeared to be about Kelly's bloke? But what did Frank know? He'd never met Kelly's boyfriend. If he was a crackhead, Nelson's beef may well be justified. Just like Frank believed his gripes about Donovan had always been warranted. Frank was pleased when a message popped up on his screen telling him there was a pile of food photos ready to be downloaded from their FTP site. He hoped the work would keep his mind off bloody Donovan, Kelly, and all the rest of them.

Kelly was jerked from slumber by the ringtone on her new mobile. She'd been meaning to change it but kept forgetting. It had to be the most annoying collection of notes ever. The only reason she could see for making it so discordant was so people would answer their phones fast, just to end the irritation. In which case, it was a clever arrangement … it worked on her. But then, when she heard Donovan's nasal drawl, she wished she'd let it ring.

"Mornin' sunshine," he said.

"What do you want?"

"I just wanted you to know I've arranged to have some photos taken of you tonight," said Donovan. "I hope you've had lots of beauty sleep."

"What you on about?" said Kelly, yawning loudly. When she sat up, the realization that she was alone in bed hit her like a punch in the guts. The bitter memory of Jason walking out after giving her hell took her breath away.

Him having taken her apart so calmly and logically, like someone on telly, made her feel worse than if he'd lost it and called her every nasty name under the sun.

Donovan babbled on.

"We're going to need some recent glam shots of you to satisfy the feeding frenzy when I tell the press you're recording some astoundingly brilliant tracks for the next album — release date in eight weeks."

The last thing Kelly needed was Donovan rattling her cage about a second album.

"Tell you what Donovan … call me back when you find your mind, 'cos you've clearly lost it, alright?"

The smart-arse answer may have come across as flippant, but Kelly was panicking — she could tell he meant what he'd said about releasing a new album.

"I just put out a press release saying how Jason's overdose was a wake-up call, and how you're cleaning up your act. MailOnline have already picked it up and the rest of the vultures will be on it by end of day."

The mention of Jason's so-called overdose had Kelly distracted, wide awake, and spitting bullets.

"About that … you spiked his bloody coffee, didn't you? What the fuck, Donovan. You could have killed him."

It wasn't until then that it dawned on Kelly that Donovan had been carrying two coffees when he pitched up in the dressing room at the Catacomb. She remembered he'd offered her one, as he sometimes did, always forgetting she didn't drink the stuff. When she refused, she was certain he'd handed the cardboard tray holding both cups to Jason. It must have been pure chance that Jason drank the nobbled one, unless …

"You fucking maniac. Both those coffees were fixed, weren't they?"

There was a slight silence on the phone before Donovan spoke, quietly for him.

"I was hoping for a double whammy. But I clean forgot about your aversion to coffee."

Kelly couldn't believe it. It was the weirdest feeling to think that she and Jason could both so easily be dead.

"Can you imagine the splash?" Donovan continued, his voice squeakier now, clearly excited. "Kelly Anton O/D-ing on stage, and her ne'er-do-well druggie boyfriend doing the same in the dressing room? It'd have been national news on all the major networks, as well as the usual trashy tabloids and web sites who ended up covering Jason's overdose anyway."

"But why?" asked Kelly, more a gasp than a question.

"For one thing you wasn't looking the part. Too alert for a crackhead. The media always say you're out of your skull, but it must be obvious to some you're really not. But with the date-rape stuff you'd have been really trashed. Which would have made your comeback so much more ... sen-fucking-sational ... coming after you were so out of it you could barely stand in front of an audience. But I suppose we'll have to make do with it just being about you seeing the light after Jason's overdose, and not after yours too."

Donovan was obviously out of his mind. Kelly could see it now. She knew she should never have gone along with his plan, but she never dreamed he'd take things so far. But what else could she have done? She had no new material, so why not explain the non-appearance of the long-promised album by making out she was too messed up to deliver the goods. She wasn't so sure if Donovan was right when he kept repeating the old chestnut about there being "no such thing as bad publicity," but there was certainly a shit load of press the few times she managed to act as if she was out of it. And she didn't really give a toss what people thought. Except for her father, who she'd stupidly not considered when she went along with

Donovan's crazy scheme. Trouble was, it was making the situation worse with her father. Christ, what a mess. At the idea of her lack of material, Kelly began to freak.

"But I haven't got a single track. How can I do a whole album?"

"That one you did at the club wasn't bad," said Donovan.

"Christ, Donovan, you saw the crowd. It went over like a cup of cold sick."

"Tart it up in the studio, it'll be fine."

As Donovan was talking, it began to dawn on Kelly what he'd said about cleaning up her act.

"Enough of all this writer's block 'drought' business," Donovan continued. "Just put your arse on a chair and get a few songs down, no more fucking excuses."

An inkling of an idea — a faint hope — was taking shape in Kelly's brain.

"In that press release you've made out I'm cleaning up my act, right?"

"Penny's finally dropped," said Donovan. "I've fixed a photographer to come to your place tonight. to do some snaps we can release once enough time has passed for you to be all rehabilitated."

Donovan laced the word with sarcasm, and then he chortled. Kelly thought he sounded truly maniacal.

"This shooter's done loads of celebrity photos, so he's used to dealing with pains in the bum like you. I want proper Vanity Fair type stuff. So, you've got to scrub up, alright? I want you looking all radiant and healthy."

"Oh right, no worries," said Kelly slowly, to buy her some time to think. "Yeah, great."

Donovan started to say something, but she cut him off.

"I mean, we can go straight into the studio if you like, but it'd be better to give me at least a few weeks first."

"No way. I want you where I can keep an eye on you," said Donovan. "And I've got Chuck Simpson booked to produce. He wasn't easy to get, so you'd better come up with some material."

"I'm telling you, Donovan, working up lyrics with the likes of Chuck in the studio would be a waste of money. Let me prepare first. Then I'll work my arse off with him to do the recording in just a couple of weeks."

Kelly was pretty sure the money angle would persuade him. She could tell it was working when Donovan didn't immediately reply.

"Okay, you've got a month before we go into the studio," he said after a pause. "But you'd better have everything ready, so we can lay a dozen or so tracks down lickety-split. There's the mixing and mastering after that, don't forget."

"I'm not promising anything Donovan. But I'll try," said Kelly, using her most goody-goody voice.

"See you tonight then. We'll be there at seven. Make sure you're all primped and beautified, okay?"

"Yeah, cool." Which was something she never usually said, but she was trying — maybe a bit too hard — to watch herself where Donovan was concerned.

After she'd rung off, Kelly settled back in the bed. She reached out a hand to feel the empty space on Jason's side. She was surprised not to feel more bereft that the sheet was cold, but her mind was in overdrive, going over the ramifications of Donovan's call. Once the press had bought his press release about her cleaning up her act — and there was no reason to think they wouldn't — there'd be no need for any more dope-head acts on her part. With her miraculous 'recovery,' and the fact that Jason wasn't around anymore, she should be able to square things with her father. They'd have four weeks before going into the studio. Which was tight, but not impossible. All a bit iffy, but what else could she do?

Kelly reached for the phone, hoping to hell the hair and make-up blokes she'd used in the past would not only remember her but take her at short notice. When they couldn't get her into their salon fast enough, she wondered why she'd ever doubted they wouldn't want to. Sometimes — less and less often, but occasionally — she forgot who she was. Or at least, who people saw her as. She hoped a few hours getting dolled up might take her mind off Jason.

FRANK WAS SURPRISED — but mightily relieved — that Kelly showed hardly a flicker of recognition when he and Donovan walked out of the private lift into her penthouse. A slight narrowing of her eyes might have given the game away, but then, after Donovan introduced him, all she said was "Pleased to meet you." Frank concluded, by the slight shake of her head as she held his gaze, that Kelly had in fact recognized him, but didn't want Donovan to know about their having met. Nor, he presumed, about his friendship with her father. All of which distracted him somewhat from the job at hand — not to mention how utterly awesome Kelly was looking.

Over the years Frank had come to the conclusion that star power — or star charisma, or whatever people wanted to call it — really did exist. Whether it was present from birth, or if it was acquired as a person rose to fame, Frank wasn't sure. When he'd met Kelly the day before, conditions hadn't been the best. She was obviously upset as soon as she appeared at her parents' kitchen door. But even in those few fraught minutes, in the dim light of a modest kitchen, Frank had seen enough to know Kelly had 'it' in spades — whatever 'it' was.

Nelson said Kelly had had her melt down and stormed off because she hadn't expected to find her father at home.

He said that since they'd had a bust up a few months previous, she only came around when the coast was clear. Nelson had been at home unexpectedly, because a gig with his band had been cancelled. Frank thought her tantrum might have had more to do with the way Nelson had dissed Kelly's boyfriend, but he kept quiet.

Kelly wasn't beautiful, at least not in any conventional way. Nose a little too wide, perhaps. But she was stunning nevertheless, as she stood at the lift door, ready to greet him and Donovan. She wore a tight, 50s-style, black taffeta skirt, which ended just below her knees. A wide black, patent leather belt cinched her waist. Her top was a simple, long-sleeved, scarlet shirt. Collar up and buttons open to reveal her snake tattoo and ample cleavage above a black, low-cut, lace-trimmed bra. Frank noticed she'd removed her eyebrow ring. He assumed to appear less hard-core aggressive, which was probably a savvy move on Kelly's part. Her shoulder-length hair curled around her neck in the loose style Frank had seen in her video. To the casual observer it may have seemed un-styled, but he could tell from the sheen and the fact that each tress fell alluringly in the exact right spot, that it had been professionally conditioned and arranged. Frank suspected there was makeup involved, but it had been so well applied the effect was simply of a healthy glow to her flawless skin. The only place make-up was evident was in the exaggerated eyeliner, extending from the corner of each eye as far as her temple. He supposed the luscious pink of her plump lips could only have come from lipstick, but it certainly wasn't in-your-face obvious.

It occurred to Frank that the clothes, hair, and makeup were secondary. Skillfully thought-out and complementary, but only packaging. It was from her eyes and her bearing that the star power blazed. Kelly's irises were paler than one might have expected, more honey than chocolate.

But it wasn't the extraordinary colour of her eyes that made such an impression on Frank. It was the emotion they evoked when she looked at him. He'd heard the thing about eyes being windows to the soul, but Kelly's were more like reflections of the observer's soul … his soul. They made him feel joyful, miserable, ecstatic, optimistic, and scared. All at the same time. The unsettling effect was heightened by her complete stillness. She regarded him without moving a muscle. Frank thought of a panther, debating if there was enough meat on his bones before making the effort to pounce.

"Come on then, David Bailey. We haven't got all bloody night," said Donovan.

Frank, having been jerked out of his reverie, looked around for a good spot to shoot. The place was sparsely furnished. And what little there was didn't match. His eye fell on a Victorian chaise longue, covered in white fabric. The only other seats were a couple of chairs, all chrome tubes and tautly stretched leather. Frank knew that the chairs were mid-century modern collectables, but they always looked uncomfortable to him. They were grouped around a wooden coffee table that appeared to be 1950s Scandinavian. No pictures on the walls. No rugs or carpet on the vast, blonde, wooden floor. The place looked like Kelly and her boyfriend had only just moved in, but Frank had been told by Donovan on the way up in the lift that they'd been there for almost a year, just after her last album had gone "diamond."

"How many do you have to sell to be 'diamond' then?" Frank had asked.

"Ten million or more," said Donovan.

Donovan looked so pleased with himself, Frank wished he hadn't asked. He certainly wasn't going to inquire how much revenue was involved, but it had to be in the hundreds of millions of pounds. Plus, all the ongoing performance rights royalties. Frank had done his best not to look impressed.

"I think we'll have you on the white chaise," said Frank to Kelly. "Just give me a couple of minutes to set up."

Kelly directed him to an electrical outlet for the equipment Donovan had brought, which was adequate. A twin kit — two lights with trigger and receiver. The camera was a good one, a Nikon with 15-88 mm lens, perfect for portraits.

When Kelly said, "I fucking hate having my photo taken," Frank thought it sounded more like a challenge than the truth. As if Kelly were saying, "prove to me you're worth my time." It was hard to believe her when she fell quite naturally into an amazing pose, having kicked off her high-heeled shoes. She sat erect, but sideways to the camera, her knees bent, and legs tucked provocatively to one side. When Frank looked in the viewfinder, Kelly turned her head to the lens, and there was that gaze — extraordinary even on the camera's tiny screen. As long as he had the lighting right, it was hard to go wrong with a subject like Kelly.

Frank hadn't done a lot of studio work. His work at the Mail, first in the dark room and then as a staff photographer, had propelled him directly into the world of a freelance paparazzo. But along the way, when people had asked, he'd hired a studio to shoot their portraits, or done it outside in natural light. He'd always enjoyed the interaction with his subjects in an atmosphere of agreeable collaboration rather than conflict, which, he had to admit, no matter what he told Ali, was more often than not the state of affairs when working as a pap. During a prearranged shoot a relationship often developed with a willing subject that felt more like seduction than work. A photographer's instructions, for example — "chin up," "turn your head slightly," "pull your legs in a little more" — sounded to

Frank like mild dominance during lovemaking. Then there were the exaggerated expressions of pleasure when things were going well. "That's good," "beautiful," "perfect!" To which the subject almost always responded with extra effort in posing, or with added intensity in their expression. Frank had often thought there was logic to the words "the camera loves her," with its vague sexual innuendo.

And Kelly, despite protestations of feeling uncomfortable, was a performer after all. She responded readily and well to Frank's prompts. He hadn't realized how much time had passed until Donovan piped up.

"I hate to interrupt, but this could go on all bloody night with you two, the rate you're going. And Whitney's threatened to have my testicles on a tray if I'm late, so I'm off."

Frank was so preoccupied with shooting he barely registered the pang of sadness he usually felt whenever his daughter's name was mentioned.

"Just leave all the gear here, alright?" said Donovan.

"I'll have to take the remote drive to download from in the morning, and it'll take an hour after that to have the heroes ready to transmit."

Frank was planning to go into the agency early to use their computer.

"Heroes?" asked Donovan.

Frank realized he'd lapsed into photographer-speak.

"The good shots, the ones you'll want to use."

"Whatever," said Donovan. "Just send them to my tekkie at Canary when they're ready."

He handed Frank a business card with a name and e-mail address, presumably that of the IT guy, written on it. He blew Kelly a kiss, to which she gave him the finger, then he headed for the lift. Frank turned his attention back to Kelly.

Frank had enough experience to know the point in a

photo shoot when he had enough choice shots in the can. Only ten minutes or so passed after Donovan left before Frank decided they were done.

"You sure you got enough?" asked Kelly.

"I think you enjoy this more than you let on," said Frank in what he hoped was a teasing voice. He was relieved when she let out a hearty belly laugh.

"It's just that you're good," she said. "You make it no-fuss, no-muss."

"Praise indeed," said Frank.

"You wanna drink?" she asked. "I think we got a beer or two in the fridge."

Frank was glad she didn't expect him to run off right away. It was good to have a bit of a breather after the intensity of the shoot.

"Just plain old London tap water for me, please," he said.

"Then you can tell me all about my grumpy old Dad," she said, as she walked toward the kitchen area.

Frank was relieved that Kelly had taken his request for water without questioning it in the way some people did. It never ceased to piss him off when people treated you like you were antisocial for not wanting alcohol. Not that Frank was above saying right out that he was an alcoholic. That usually shut them up.

"What do you want to know about your Dad?" asked Frank, when they were settled on the chrome chairs at the coffee table. Frank found the chair more comfortable than he'd imagined, once he slid into its polished leather seat.

"First of all, I want to know what the fuck you're doing with Donovan," said Kelly, more of a fierce accusation than a question.

The atmosphere had changed in an instant from cosy chat to tense interrogation. During the shoot Frank had forgotten his concern about her recognizing him and subsequent relief that she hadn't acknowledged him. It was only natural that she'd be wondering what the hell his connection to Donovan was.

"He's my son-in-law," said Frank. "That's all."

"You're 'aving a laugh," said Kelly. "You expect me to believe you just happen to pitch up at my Dad's house, and then — oh, what a surprise — here you are doing a photo session with me for Donovan … you son-in-law. My Mum said you was a good bloke, despite that fake photo stunt you pulled on my Dad when you and him were young."

Frank was amazed she knew about the student newspaper photograph. He could only assume Ruth had told her all the ins and outs of it after she'd taken off after Kelly the day before.

"But you can't blame me for wondering if you and Donovan are up to something," Kelly continued. "Tell me straight, Frank, what the fuck's going on?"

Frank tried to reassure Kelly there was no funny business happening by telling her his whole sad story. How his daughter had married Donovan. He outlined briefly his so-called assault, the court case, and its outcome. He told her about running into Donovan on the bus, how he realized he'd been tricked by him into going to the club with Ali to take photos so Donovan would have something over on him.

"The little bleeder certainly loves manipulating people," said Kelly.

Something about the forlorn way she said it made Frank suspect she was speaking from personal experience.

"No offence Frank, but it's not like somebody like you can do much for him, is there?"

"He's made me do this shoot," said Frank, somewhat defensively. "But I have to admit it seems like he went to a lot of trouble just to have something over on me."

"Actually, he probably doesn't need a reason. He's just a fucking psychopath, end of."

"I was glad you didn't let on you'd already met me. The less Donovan knows the better, as far as I'm concerned," said Frank.

"You've never told him you're my Dad's old mate?"

"Not at all. I didn't know myself 'til yesterday."

Frank was relieved that she seemed reassured by his story. She certainly appeared less scrappy. He'd been quite scared when she'd fixed him with her honeyed eyes, less liquid and a lot more flinty than during the shoot.

"But hang about, you mean to say you never knew my Dad was your old pal when you went to the house with that lad you work with, what took the photos?"

"No idea, I swear," said Frank. "It was honestly pure coincidence. I was floored, honest. I still can't get my head around it."

"When exactly did you and my Dad meet, anyway?" she asked.

"Summer of 1967."

Kelly whistled, presumably at the early date.

She adopted a patois lilt. "'ow yuh two meetin'? A young negah from Jamrock an' a white bwoy like yuh."

Frank laughed, as much with relief that the atmosphere had reverted back to friendly as at her convincing Jamaican accent. He described the building site just outside Wolverhampton where he'd met Nelson. He talked about the long grueling hours they'd worked, telling her it hadn't been so bad for him as a casual summer labourer, but how tough it must have been for Nelson, working five-and-a-half days a week, year in year out, often far from home. Especially in the winters, when he would have felt the cold to his bones.

Maybe he laid it on a bit thick, but he thought a daughter should know about a father's hard times. He wished Whitney had listened when he tried to tell her about the years of hard graft he'd put in at the Mail and for the years after. But maybe that stuff needed to come from a third party to get a daughter's attention. When Frank mentioned Nelson's Auntie Irene, with whom Nelson was living back when they met, Kelly grilled him about her.

"I wish I'd met her before she died, she sounds like a live-wire. I only ever saw the two remaining Jamaican aunts, when we were at my Dad's house in Jamaica last year."

"Nelson has a house in Jamaica?"

"Well, I bought it for him," said Kelly, looking surprisingly bashful.

"That house of theirs in Battersea must be worth a bundle now," said Frank, a weak attempt to take the focus off Kelly's obvious sheepishness.

"Ye-ah," said Kelly, in exaggerated agreement. "Good job they paid for it years ago. I couldn't afford to buy it for them now, price of property round there."

Frank thought it was an odd thing for a 'diamond' recording artist to claim. He'd have thought she could afford to buy half of Nelson's street, never mind a single house.

Kelly was clearly amazed when Frank told her about Nelson spending time in prison, even if it was only a few days.

"Bugger me," she said. "My discreet lawyer mother left that little detail out of the story. Although she told me he could have been done for murder, right?"

"If your mother and I hadn't been able to prove that he wasn't in Wolverhampton when the Sikh landlord was attacked," said Frank. "So, he couldn't have done it."

As a guilty afterthought, Frank added, "My girlfriend, now my wife, helped too."

"Wow," said Kelly.

"Ex-wife, I should say," said Frank.

There was a silence. Frank's thoughts, having mentioned when he and Christine were first together, were filled with nostalgia. It struck him how quiet Kelly's penthouse was. He supposed it was the elevation, far above the London hurly burly. He glanced at Kelly, who was staring into space.

"Your Dad's really worried about you, you know," he said.

"For fuck's sake Frank. Just as you and me was getting along so well."

Frank grimaced. He knew he'd be taking a chance, but he'd promised Nelson he'd do whatever he could to put Kelly on the straight and narrow. Although at the time — sitting around Nelson and Ruth's kitchen table — he hadn't known the opportunity would arise so soon. He couldn't blow it now. He tried another tactic.

"Although I have to say, now I've seen you up close and personal, so to speak, it's hard to believe all that stuff about you being off your head and …"

"Donovan said you was a big press photographer, right?"

Kelly had interrupted him so abruptly, trying to establish his credentials, it seemed to Frank she was deciding whether to trust him with something or other.

"I was, yes," he said. "Before my paparazzo days."

The minute the words were out of his mouth he worried his revelation would alienate Kelly, but she didn't seem phased.

"So, you should know you can't believe hardly anything your read in the papers."

Frank was relieved she hadn't pounced on the paparazzo mention.

"I know. Believe me, I know more than anyone. But there've been videos and photos … you and your boyfriend, both trashed. Even Donovan goes on about it."

Kelly shook her head. Frank was pleased to see she didn't appear angry. She observed him steadily, the way people do in an argument when they believe they know more than you do and are tempted to say it but aren't sure if they should. She took a breath and said, "I tell you Frank, the whole thing has been Donovan's loony tunes idea."

"What whole thing?" asked Frank.

Kelly examined him with her remarkable eyes. He'd rarely in his life felt so scrutinized. He could tell it was touch and go if she'd confide in him, spill whatever beans there were to spill.

"The truth is, Frank, I've hit a bit of a blockage, you might say," said Kelly. "A creative blockage."

"Okay," he said, hoping like hell he sounded encouraging, reassuring.

Kelly slid a little more into the leather chair, as though making herself more comfortable. She explained how, after the super-success of her album, her world went bananas.

"Honest, Frank, it was fucking nuts. Don't get me wrong, it was great to have all that approval. It's what every musician dreams of, no matter what they say. But somewhere along the way, I just froze up."

"You mean stage fright," said Frank. He had in mind the look on Kelly's face in the Catacomb as she fled the stage.

"Not so much. More about being super aware that I couldn't put a single decent track together for a second album. And all these expectations are piling up. And the worst of them was from Donovan. He kept pushing and pushing."

"Alright," said Frank, trying his best to sound sympathetic. He supposed making a second album — or book or film, come to that — on the heels of a mega hit must be daunting, to say the least.

"In the end Donovan brings up this photo that some fucking pap — sorry, a 'press photographer' — had snapped of Jason and me coming out of a club. Jason was pretty smashed. But I swear, Frank, I was stone cold sober, straight as could be. I'm like my Dad that way. I get sick if I drink more than a couple, and drugs scare the shit out of me. I'm too much of a control freak to give myself up to them. It's just that the shot they used was one of those bloody awful eyes-half-closed ones where even a fucking nun would look squiffy if snapped at the wrong moment, like I was. They publish this photo with a caption claiming me and Jason are both out of our trees. The weather was tropical at the time, so to stay cool all I was wearing was a shitty old vest and a pair of frayed cut-offs. I have to admit I looked a right mess."

Kelly sounded straight-up. And how many times had Frank seen photos — especially those with captions dreamed up by an over-excited editor — that totally misrepresented a situation? Just like the one she'd described.

"My Dad was already peeved about me being with Jason 'cos some great-great uncle of his was a slave trader, or some shit. So, when the photo first appeared, and after my Dad saw it and read the caption, him and I had this massive barney. Nothing I could say would persuade him I wasn't up to my eyeballs in drugs."

Kelly stopped talking abruptly. She looked away.

"I don't know why I mentioned that. My Dad's got fuck-all to do with it."

She appeared distracted somehow, staring into space for a second or two.

"Where was I? Oh, yeah. Then Donovan tells me the photo that started all the bother with my Dad had pulled in more attention — hits on the web, press stories, blah, blah — than most others where I was just me, normal like. Donovan reckoned I should make out I'm trashed now and again."

Kelly wriggled uncomfortably in her chair.

"I know it sounds fucking nuts, but you wouldn't believe how easy it was to lure the bastards into taking pictures of me."

"Actually," said Frank. "I can well believe it."

"There were loads of times when one or more paps would show up outside some club or other, without them knowing it was me who'd tipped them off from inside. Donovan had given me numbers for a load of them. I just made out when I called that I was a regular customer at whichever place we were at, I told them Kelly Anton was there and out of her tree. It worked a treat. When me and Jason staggered out, flashes were popping off faster than strobes. Our photos were plastered all over the tabloids the very next morning. I scammed them paps six ways to Sunday, so it'd be a bit rich for me to get all high and mighty about them. I saw how scared you looked when you let slip you'd been one."

Frank smiled and put his hands up in mock surrender that she'd seen through him.

"Donovan started putting it about that I'm in no fit state," Kelly continued. "He said the whole shebang would explain the delay on the album while still keeping up the publicity. Then, when I came up with the goods for some tracks, he'd issue an official press release that I've cleaned up my act. And, hey presto, another brilliant release that everyone will be gagging to hear, to find out if it's really any good."

Kelly ran out of steam. She uncrossed her legs and settled back in her chair. Frank's mind was all over the place. He realized Kelly was probably self-centred — most performers are, after all — but Frank wouldn't have pegged her as callous. He didn't think she'd have gone along with Donovan's idea without considering how upset Nelson would be. Also, she didn't strike Frank as being so fragile as to be paralyzed by the pressure to produce a follow-up album. He very much doubted that a musician who could produce the track he'd seen her perform would suddenly dry up. He was convinced there was something Kelly was keeping to herself.

"Say something, Frank. The suspense is killing me."

"First off, you can't blame your Dad if he gets upset about your living with a crackhead. Not exactly what anybody'd wish for a daughter, is it?"

Kelly let out a whoosh of air. She was clearly trying to keep her cool.

"Jason smokes the occasional pipe. He's no crackhead. I can't tell you how many times I've tried to explain to my father that it's no worse than his mates' ganja habit."

"What about his overdose, just the other day. Don't tell me that was nothing."

Kelly let out a hollow laugh. Frank had never heard anything more mirthless. She told him such an outrageous story he wondered for a second if she was the unhinged one and not Donovan.

"You're telling me Donovan slipped Jason date-rape drug. And you would have had some too, except he forgot you don't like coffee? I'm sorry, Kelly, but I just don't believe it — even of Donovan."

"Jason will back me up, and if we really had to prove it, I expect the hospital has it all in their records," said Kelly, so defiantly that Frank wavered.

"Jesus, maybe he is off his fucking nut."

He hoped Whitney was safe, living with a psycho.

"He even had a weird justification for it," said Kelly. "Said I needed to look drugged. He made out people were beginning to guess I wasn't really out of my tree at all."

Frank thought back to the Catacomb and how he'd had his suspicion she was more anxious than drugged when she fled the stage in such a hurry. But then another thought occurred to him.

"I'm no music fan, Kelly, but if I was, I'd be royally pissed off if I found out my idol had been pulling the wool over my eyes, acting like a druggie, then turns out they they wasn't at all. Just for a bit of extra publicity."

"I know, I know," said Kelly.

"But apart from the effect on fans, it's downright slimy. And it's downright cruel to your Dad. I'm willing to bet you didn't tell him your so-called drug habit was all show."

"Honest, Frank, I couldn't. Donovan leant on me not tell a soul and I had no option but to go along with Donovan's scheme."

Frank remembered how Kelly had sounded when she'd talked about Donovan's manipulating people. As if she had more than just a passing acquaintance with his tactics.

"There's got to be something you're not telling me," said Frank. "I don't believe you'd have just gone along with Donovan's nut-bar scheme 'cos you thought it was a good idea. You've got more to you than that."

Kelly let out a long exhalation.

"You're a fly one, aren't you, Frank. Truth is, I owe him money. A shitload of money. He hasn't just got me over a barrel, he's got me inside the fucking thing."

"How can you owe him money? If anything, he must owe you, for Christ's sake."

"After I bought this place — which was mainly his doing but never mind, eh? It was around the same time I bought the place in Jamaica for my folks. Which cost nothing compared to London property prices, but it took the advance Donovan had paid me before the album was released. Donovan said he'd lend me the sale price for this place until the album royalties were in my bank. It takes forever sometimes. But when he eventually sat me down to go over the financials on the album, it turned out it didn't do as well as you might think. I hadn't earned enough to pay for the bleeding penthouse. I was all for re-selling it there and then, but Donovan talked me out of it. He said Canary would bankroll me against the next album."

Frank could see Kelly was becoming upset. Not quite crying — he doubted she was the tearful type — but close enough.

169

"Which of course just added to the fucking pressure to produce something," she said.

"Look, Kelly, something's not right. If that album sold more than ten million copies, you must have earned enough to buy half-a-dozen penthouses."

"This place cost four million, Frank. Four million fucking pounds," said Kelly, a little too emphatically for Frank's liking. As if he wouldn't know how much a riverside penthouse cost. But then he wondered if perhaps it showed that Kelly herself had no idea about money, and the worth of things.

"And I don't think the album sold as many as ten million."

"That's what Donovan told me," said Frank.

"He was probably bragging."

"But even if it sold half that many, you'd still be in clover."

"You've no idea, Frank, how much it takes to record, promote, and all that stuff. And being on tour costs a frigging fortune. All them roadies, and travel expenses."

"I'm sure. But put against what you earn in revenue from each gig, there must be a massive profit."

Kelly shook her head resignedly.

"I've seen the figures, Frank. I'm telling you it's not as much as you might think."

Frank supposed she must be right, but, given Donovan's deviousness, he wouldn't be surprised if there wasn't something dodgy about the way Kelly's slice of the pie had been cut. Until he knew better, he thought he'd better drop the subject.

"Where is Jason anyway? I'd have thought he might be intrigued to see a master photographer at work."

"We've split up," said Kelly. "I told him about my part in Donovan's scheme and he just took off. Can't say I blame him."

She seemed so small and fragile, sitting in the brutal

chrome and leather framework of the modernistic chair, that Frank's paternal tendencies threatened to overwhelm him.

"He didn't know?"

"Not 'til I told him. Jason had had the shit kicked out of his character by them newspaper twats more than once," said Kelly. "So ,when I admitted to him that I'd encouraged them ..."

Her voice trailed off. Frank didn't know what to say. He thought about how many breakups he might have been responsible for when he was one of the 'newspaper twats' that Kelly had mentioned.

"Sorry to hear," he said, knowing it sounded lame.

Kelly seemed to pull herself together. She stood up.

"Do me a favour. Make sure you let my Dad know Jason's gone. It sounds like I'm a cold bitch, but I may as well use his leaving to stop him being so bloody stubborn."

"Will do," said Frank, pulling himself out of his chair. He didn't really understand exactly what Nelson was being stubborn about. Not giving Kelly the benefit of the doubt when she insisted she wasn't a drug user, he supposed.

"And try and persuade him I've not got track marks up both my arms. Tell him how the frigging media works, and that all them reports are bullshit."

She seemed incredibly young, staring at Frank with her pleading limpid eyes. If it wasn't for the eye liner, she'd have looked about sixteen years old. She reminded Frank of Whitney when she was a kid. He had to say though, he didn't remember Whitney appearing quite so desperate, even when she beseeched Frank to be more accepting of Donovan.

"Good to see how much you want to get back in your Dad's good books."

"You don't know the half of it, Frank," said Kelly.

"I'll do my best to talk you up," said Frank, and, before

he had a chance to think, he kissed her on the forehead.

As he descended in the lift, Frank thought how he couldn't wait to tell Ali that he'd kissed Kelly Anton goodnight and watch the lad turn green with envy.

It wasn't until a good half-hour after Frank had left that Kelly realized she'd spent the whole time since just pacing from one end of the penthouse to the other, her arms wrapped around herself. Now and then she stopped to gaze out of one of the walls of glass, but for all she took in of the panorama of city lights stretching as far as the horizon, she may as well have been staring at a blank wall.

"Fuck it," she said loudly, and strode into the bedroom, unbuckling her belt and unbuttoning her blouse. She shrugged off her top, unzipped her skirt, and stepped out if it. But her decisiveness drained away as quickly as it had engulfed her. She stood looking around, wondering what the hell to do next. She rummaged in the bottom of a cupboard and, without really knowing what she was looking for, she glommed on to a 'vintage' tracksuit Jason had triumphantly rooted out from a mound of new arrivals at a thrift shop. Kelly remembered how he crowed about what a find it had been for only five pounds. It was Adidas, she knew from the logo, and Jason had gone on about some German footballer or other who'd worn one just like it back in the '70s. As Kelly pulled it on, she caught a whiff of Jason's anti-perspirant. It was the first time she'd come close to tears since he'd left. The tracksuit wasn't polyester like the shell suits every grime artist in East London had started wearing, but a kind of brushed cotton. Despite the feeling brought on by the smell — that Jason could be standing next to her — Kelly found the softness of the fabric comforting, if bittersweet. She tried to kid herself she'd only been feeling a bit fragile because she was cold.

Kelly may have felt less untethered, but with her settling came an overwhelming sense of loneliness. She wasn't used to spending time on her own. Since she met Jason they'd barely been out of each other's sight. The only time they'd been apart had been for the six weeks when she was on tour promoting the album. Apart from her mother, she hadn't had a good chinwag with anybody else for ages. She hadn't talked to Sharon, her bezzie mate from school, for months.

"Jesus, Kelly, d'you know what time it is?" asked Sharon, sounding sleepy when she picked up the phone.

"Oh, sorry, is it late?"

"Maybe not for a night-owl superstar like you, but I'm on a double shift at work tomorrow. I'll be crawling out of bed at half-past five."

Sharon worked at a call centre on the Isle of Dogs, next-door to Tower Hamlets where she'd moved when she got married, a few years back. Kelly could probably see the building where Sharon worked from her east-facing windows.

"What you pushing this week, then?" asked Kelly.

"Insurance, it's a fucking nightmare."

"Do you have to put on an Indian accent to work there?" asked Kelly.

She thought it was a hilarious question, given that almost every call centre she'd ever phoned was obviously somewhere like the Punjab or New Delhi, judging from the voices on the other end.

"What you on about?" asked Sharon. "And to what do I owe this honour, anyway?"

"Nothing, just called to see how you were doing."

"Levon was laid off, so I'm taking on extra shifts, which you'd think was doable with him looking after the kids all day, but he's clueless. Yesterday he put Susie's pink 'Barbie' T-shirt on Alan and sent him off to school. Poor kid was teased rotten."

Kelly could hear a male voice, presumably Levon. It sounded like he was objecting to Sharon dissing his parenting skills. Kelly imagined them lying in bed next to each other.

"Jason and me broke up," said Kelly.

There was a silence, during which Kelly began to feel guilty. She knew Sharon had it tough. And worse now, with her husband out of work. Waking her up and whining about her posh boyfriend leaving her seemed downright selfish, especially when Kelly had brought it on herself.

"Kelly love, I'm so sorry. But I gotta get some kip. I'll try you on my lunch break tomorrow, okay. We can chat."

"Yeah, yeah, of course," said Kelly, "Sleep tight."

Kelly sunk into the mattress and pulled the duvet over her head.

She woke up God knows how much time later and reached out to turn off the bedside light that she'd left on. Despite the semi-darkness, the longer she lay, now totally awake, the more she stewed about Donovan. She ran a whole scenario in her head, vivid as watching a movie, about what she'd do to expose the little fucker.

First thing in the morning she'd get in touch with one of the breakfast talk shows, there was that new one on BBC, and organize an interview. She'd wear what she wore for the photoshoot and tell the millions watching about Donovan's ruse, her part in it, exactly what she did, and how sorry she is to all her fans for pulling the wool over their eyes. She dictated in her head exactly what she'd say, sometimes repeating it a few times to get just the right emphasis. One that would paint Donovan in the worst light possible.

She knew she'd have no trouble selling BBC on an interview if she said she planned to make a sensational confession. Who knows? If she called early enough and said she could be at the studio right away, they might air it there and then. Although, for maximum viewers, they'd probably want to publicize it ahead of time. But she could wait a day, couldn't she?

"WHO KICKED YOU out of bed then?" asked Cheryl, the receptionist, when Frank arrived at FoodFoto at half-past-eight, a good half-an-hour before his usual start time.

"Sophia Loren," he shot back, as he breezed past her to the basement stairs.

"You wish," Frank heard Cheryl shout, as he descended to the bowels of the agency.

Once he'd transferred the previous evening's photos of Kelly from the remote drive to his computer, he started trolling through to choose a couple of the best ones. He congratulated himself on his decision to put Kelly on the chaise. The combination of black skirt and red blouse against white linen upholstery was startlingly graphic. Almost every frame could have been a candidate for a cover image on any of the glossies. Kelly, of course, looked amazing. There was hardly a frame where she wasn't engaged with the camera. Frank always prided himself as a swift and accurate editor, but he was finding it difficult to choose — every single shot was a winner. After twenty minutes or so he'd managed to narrow it down to three. He e-mailed the IT guy at Canary Records with the winners attached, telling him if he wanted any at a higher resolution to call and Frank would arrange to have them put on an FTP site.

After the e-mail showed up in his sent folder, Frank thought he'd feel more relieved, having done everything Donovan had demanded. But he was still aware of a cloud of uncertainty hovering over him. It must be how everybody felt when they were being blackmailed. Never knowing, even after the latest demand is met, if they're really free. The thought occurred to him that perhaps he should just go to the police, or the court, or wherever, to make a clean breast of having gone to the Catacomb. Maybe if he explained how he'd been manipulated by Donovan into going to the club they'd go easy on him ... but Frank discounted the idea almost before it was formed. After all, it could go badly. They wouldn't give a shit if he'd been coerced and he'd end up in jail.

"Wow! Khoobsurat!"

"Bloody hell, Ali, you scared the shit out of me, creeping up and shouting Pakistani words in my ear hole."

Ali was leaning so far over Frank's shoulder he was in danger of falling into the computer screen, where one of the photos of Kelly was enlarged.

"It's Urdu — no such thing as Pakistani."

"Whatever," said Frank. He rolled his chair away to give Ali room to go through all the shots. He ooh-ed and ah-ed at every one.

"You're good, man. You ought to do this professionally," said Ali.

"Very funny."

"Mind you, hard to go wrong with Kelly Anton, innit."

"Me and Kelly are really tight now," said Frank. "I kissed her goodnight when I left."

"Fuck off."

"God's truth," said Frank. "Now, you fuck off and let me do some work."

Half-way through the morning Ali's extension rang.

"Oh, yeah, hello Mr Clarke," said Ali, emphasizing the

name for Frank's benefit. Frank turned to look.

"I'm fine thanks. You?"

Ali put on a puzzled expression and shook his head at Frank, as if to ask what the hell was going on.

"Right, yeah, no worries … Nelson."

More puzzled looks and head shaking.

"Yeah, he's right here, hold on."

Ali clicked a button to put the call on hold.

"It's Kelly's Dad, being all friendly like," he said. "Told me to call him Nelson. What's that about?"

"He loves you, Ali," said Frank.

"Yeah, well, now he wants to talk to you."

Nelson was calling to ask Frank if he'd come along to see his band performing at a pub in Brixton that evening.

"An' I got a surprise for yuh, Frank. It look like yuh need cheering up when I see yuh t'other day."

He wouldn't say more, just urged Frank to come along.

"And bring that bwoy wi' yuh, if he want come," said Nelson, just before he rang off.

"You want to go to see your new best friend — Nelson — and his band in a Brixton pub tonight?" Frank asked Ali.

"Reggae band in a Brixton pub?" said Ali, in the tone of voice that suggested he'd rather slit his wrists. But after a few seconds, he said, "We'll need to take Rash with us."

The Brixton 'pub,' as Nelson had called it, turned out to be much different from what Frank had imagined. He supposed he'd had in mind the West Indian hang-out in Wolverhampton, where he sometimes went as a student back in the '60s. The place had been a make-shift dive, housed in a series of sheds with concrete floors and corrugated iron roofs. A stack of wooden crates formed a rough bar, where the only booze available were bottles of Red Stripe beer. The Brixton place was almost at the other end of the spectrum. A well-stocked, mirrored bar ran along the back wall of a vast high-ceilinged room.

177

Judging from the forest of light fixtures hovering above a large stage, the place was well rigged for major light shows. The club's entranceway walls were plastered with posters and photographs that featured musicians who'd performed there. Frank had never heard of any of them, but Ali and Rashid seemed to approve. They pointed excitedly at various photos.

"Mamadou Cissoko! And look, Rash, Amaziah," said Ali.

It cost five pounds each to get in, which Nelson had neglected to mention. Frank supposed it was only right to spend some of the money from the sale of the photos of Kelly at the Catacomb to support Nelson's band. Frank was amazed to see at least a couple hundred people inside the club. He had no idea Nelson and his band were so popular. When he said as much to Ali, Rashid pointed out that the main act was a singer called Little Roy.

"Been singing the same hit song for years, but he's still a massive reggae star," said Rashid.

"Kelly's Dad's lot must be the opening act," said Ali.

Nevertheless, Frank was impressed. He'd thought Nelson just got together with a couple of friends for an occasional jam session. Being an opening band in a place like this was a far bigger deal than Frank had imagined for Nelson and his mates. They'd no sooner bought drinks — diet coke for Frank, and coconut water for Ali and Rashid — than Nelson and his band sauntered onto the stage, looking cool. Frank was pleased when whistles and cheers from the audience greeted them. They clearly had a number of fans in the room. Nelson looked very dapper in a black and white striped shirt, black jeans, and a black fedora almost covering his white curls. He didn't look like he'd gained a pound since he and Frank were in their twenties. He took his place at a keyboard. The singer was a tall skinny man with a massive red, yellow, green and black striped beanie, which clearly held voluminous dreads.

Most numbers they played were covers of songs by Bob Marley, Jimmy Cliff, Peter Tosh, and a few Frank had never heard before. But then the singer announced a song by "our own Nelson Clarke, entitled 'You Gotta Love.'" Some of the crowd whistled and cheered in recognition. As the number continued, the words sounded familiar to Frank, but he was sure he'd never heard the song before. But, when it came to the beginning of the chorus — Some do their best to change you, Even rearrange you — he immediately remembered the lines from a song that Nelson had written and sung to him almost forty years before. It had become a bit of an ear worm for Frank back then. It was a joke between them when young Frank had begged Nelson to stop, but he'd carried right on singing it over and again. It was little wonder Frank remembered it, although with full musical accompaniment it had taken him a couple of minutes. Hearing it in a more polished form somehow seemed painfully indicative of the amount of water that had flowed under the bridge since he first heard it. Frank surreptitiously wiped a single tear from his face, hoping Ali and Rashid wouldn't notice. The group's last number was also announced as one of Nelson's. It was a rousing, upbeat song about the euphoria you feel when you know the person you love loves you back. Not exactly an original sentiment, but the arrangement was incredibly catchy. It was clear that half the audience were familiar with the song, belting out the chorus whenever it popped up. Much hooting, whistling and cheering accompanied Nelson's group as they left the stage. People shook Nelson's hand or slapped him on the back as he made his way toward Frank and the lads.

"Come, we go to the pub next door where we hear ourself talk," said Nelson. "If me stay and hear Little Roy sing 'Bongo Nyah' one mo' time, me goin' to kill meself."

This seemed to be the funniest thing Ali and Rashid

had ever heard. They cracked up. But they opted to stay, saying they might join Frank and Nelson later. Nelson seemed genuinely disappointed and urged them to come when they'd had enough of Little Roy.

"Me never understand why that man popular so," Nelson said to Frank, as they made their way out of the club. Frank smiled. He didn't remember Nelson as being competitive.

Nelson hesitated at the entrance to the pub, his hand on the door handle.

"Nah, Frank, there's a man in here yuh might not be happy to see. But don't go off on one. I 'member how yuh get."

Frank had no idea what the hell Nelson meant by either statement. Who could the unwelcome man possibly be? And what did he mean by 'how yuh get,' as Nelson had phrased it?

"Yuh promise yuh keep cool?"

"I promise," said Frank. And then as Nelson pushed the door open, he added, "Depending."

Nelson gave him a pursed-lip, disapproving grimace.

Almost the first person Frank noticed sitting a few tables away — probably because the man was staring toward the door like a rabbit frozen with fear in the headlights of a fast approaching lorry — was Jim Healey, the saxophonist, who was the supposed 'victim' when Frank was found guilty of ABH. Frank stopped abruptly.

"Believe me, Frank," said Nelson, his hand putting pressure on the small of Frank's back. "Yuh goin' to want to hear what him have to say."

As Frank sat down, Jim Healey put his pint beer glass to his lips, but more as if drinking out of nervousness than because he was thirsty.

"I see you have no trouble lifting your glass," said Frank. "I thought I'd fucked up your hand so bad you couldn't use it."

Jim had the good grace to look shamefaced.

"Now Frank, be nice," said Nelson. He went to the bar to buy drinks.

"Nelson got a hold of me," said Jim Healey.

The day Frank and Ali had turned up on Nelson's doorstep, and after Ruth had gone after Kelly, Frank had recounted to Nelson over the kitchen table the story of his court case and his suspended sentence. The music world was small enough, but throw in the fact that Jim Healey was Jamaican as well as a sax player, and it came as no surprise to Frank when Nelson said he knew him. But he never dreamt Nelson would bring them together. What the fuck for? Was it Nelson's idea of some kind of truth and reconciliation session?

"That day you beat the shit out of me ... it was all Donovan Carter's idea," Jim Healey suddenly blurted.

Frank frowned and stared at the saxophonist, struggling to take in his startling statement.

"Donovan offered me a bunch of money if I could make you clobber me. He also promised me a chance at a recording contract with Canary."

Nelson arrived from the bar with a diet coke and a pint of Guinness. He sat in the chair between Frank and Jim.

"You mean Donovan told you to wait outside my house and then make out I was trying to snap you? Get into a scuffle with me?"

"S'right," said Jim." And he arranged for them other two to be there to photograph you hitting me … and to call the police."

Frank looked at Nelson, who raised his eyebrows, pursed his lips, and shook his head, as if to say, 'incredible, but true.' Frank looked back at Jim, who held his gaze, unblinking. Frank strained to think why Donovan would possibly have gone to such lengths.

"Never dreamt you'd beat the livin' daylights outa me," said Jim.

He appeared forlorn, sitting with his shoulders hunched. Frank was surprised when he felt a glimmer of pity for him. Jim Healey had caused Frank's divorce, his estrangement from Whitney, and his bankruptcy. He ought to be punching him again, not feeling sympathetic. But Frank supposed Jim had only been a witless flunky for Donovan.

"Let me guess," Frank said to Jim. "Donovan never came through with any recording contract?"

"How did you know?" asked Jim.

Frank shook his head and asked himself if he was really so very different from Jim Healey, now that Donovan had one over on him. He'd been an idiot to take his son-in-law's bait and go to Kelly Anton's gig, break the terms of his suspended sentence. But then it dawned on Frank — giving him more hope than he'd had for years — that Jim Healey had handed him a golden opportunity to turn the tables. Maybe he should thank the poor bastard.

T ELEVISION BREAKFAST SHOWS had all finished by the time Kelly woke up. And in the light of day, her idea of revealing the whole Donovan subterfuge on live TV didn't seem like the brainwave she'd thought it was. Or was it just that she didn't have the guts to pick up the phone and make it happen? In the middle of the night she'd seen the interview clearly, like a video in her head. And it would have been the least she could have done for Jason, to put it on record that he wasn't a crackhead and that his overdose wasn't what it appeared to be. But languishing in bed, the light flooding in from floor-to-ceiling windows, Kelly told herself it was better to let Donovan put it around that she'd cleaned up her act. Then, if Frank could square things with her Dad, surely things would get back to normal, whatever the fuck normal was. Nevertheless, she was left feeling gutted that she'd copped out of what had seemed like a way to get back into Jason's good books.

When Sharon kept her promise and phoned from the call centre during her lunch break, Kelly was so relieved to hear her old friend's voice she had to gulp a few times to stop from sobbing down the phone. And Sharon's yarns about Levon's hopelessness at looking after their two kids soon had Kelly laughing.

"The other day," said Sharon. "I'm on my way out the door to work and Levon starts complaining about how they're at him all day long to play with them. I say to tell them he's busy and they've got to play on their own. They play good together if you leave them to get on with it. But then, just before I slammed the front door, I yell, 'Just let them chill.' All fucking day I'm thinking I'll get home and find he's put them in the bleeding fridge."

"He's not that clueless," said Kelly, between giggles. "Is he?"

"I wouldn't put it past him. The other day we was out of laundry detergent so he only went and used washing-up liquid in the washer, silly bugger. When I got home you couldn't get in the kitchen for bubbles and foam."

The only time Sharon mentioned Jason was just before she rung off.

"I liked Jason, I really did," she said. "But you have to admit, Kell, he was never going to be one of us, was he?"

As much as she loved her friend, Kelly knew that Sharon didn't really know Jason, she'd only met him a couple of times. And not only was Sharon dissing Jason's posh background, she made it sound like he was dead.

"Anyway, look, I gotta get back to the sweat shop. Chin up, talk to you soon."

And with that Sharon was gone.

Kelly looked around at the empty penthouse and thought about how it hadn't been long — since before her album took off — that Kelly was doing the same shit jobs as Sharon, in between the occasional paying gig. Nevertheless, Kelly wondered if she herself still qualified as 'one of us,' as Sharon had phrased it. And if not, what the fuck was she one of?

Later that evening Kelly was lounging on the white sofa thingy, as she always referred to it. She couldn't bring herself to say 'chaise longue.' Even 'chaise' on its own sounded way too stuck-up. She'd only bought the bloody thing because they needed something to sit on apart from the two modern chairs that Jason had brought from his place after he became exasperated with the lack of seating.

"They're Bauhaus, darling. You can't find better design," Jason had said, matter-of-factly, when Kelly said she didn't think they looked very comfortable.

She'd been in a hurry when she saw the chaise in the window of a shop on King's Road. She'd dashed in and bought it there and then. She could never get her head around the time and effort people took to 'decorate'. After she'd lived in the penthouse for a couple of weeks and done nothing to it, her mother suggested she hire an interior designer.

"I don't really agree with it," Ruth had said. "It smacks of elitism. But, bloody hell, Kelly, you've got to sit on something, and if you can't make the effort you may as well pay someone to do it for you."

Kelly had bought the chaise the next day, thinking she'd solved the problem. Donovan broke the news about her disappointing earnings a few days later. After his bad news, she didn't think she could have afforded a designer even if she'd wanted one.

Her phone rang — the annoying ring tone. Kelly cursed herself for having forgotten to change it. It wasn't like she didn't have the time, there was bugger-all else to do. She was so bored she'd have talked to anyone, so she didn't even check the caller ID.

"Kelly?" Jason's voice.

Her immediate thought was that he must be calling to arrange when he could have his chairs picked up.

"Who else?" she said. "It's the butler's day off."

Jason didn't respond. Why the fuck had she made such a lame joke?

"Jason," she said, when he still didn't speak.

"Can I come round?" he finally asked. His voice sounded odd, strained.

"Of course."

"See you in a bit."

He rung off.

Twenty minutes later her buzzer sounded. Kelly could see Jason on the intercom screen. As she let him in, she thought how typical it was of him not to take it for granted he could use his key. She hoped it was more from consideration for her rather than a sign of him not wanting her to think he was back living there. When he walked off the lift Kelly was shocked. She'd never seen him looking so bad. He was even paler than normal, his skin looked chalky. And his eyes were narrow and red-rimmed. Her immediate thought was that he'd been on a bender of some description — booze, or crack.

"You all right?" she asked.

Jason exhaled loudly, a heartfelt sigh.

"Not really. Jonny died."

"Fuck Jason, why didn't you say?" asked Kelly, meaning why hadn't he told her on the phone.

"I believe I just did," he said.

Kelly realized she'd have to treat him with kid gloves.

"Sorry, Jase. You want to talk about it? What happened?"

"Ironically, he was taken to St Thomas' Hospital. He

could well have been in the very same room as I was ... if he'd ever reached a room. He died in the ambulance."

"Overdose?"

Jason laughed. Such a bleak laugh, Kelly thought it was probably worse than if he'd started to cry.

"Nitrous Oxide."

"The stuff you put in fucking balloons?"

"Ridiculous, isn't it?" said Jason. "We were all at a party earlier, at Diana's."

Kelly had met Jason and Jonny's friend, Diana, once or twice. She was actually Lady Diana Somebody-Double-barreled. But Kelly liked her, she was mad.

"We'd had a bit to drink, and there were loads of other goodies too. Diana had balloons everywhere. And one of those cylinders of stuff to blow them up. Jonny and some of them started inhaling from the cylinder and talking weird, the way people do. But after a while Jonny and a couple of the others passed out. By the time anyone thought to call an ambulance, it was too late. The others were okay, but Jonny didn't make it."

Kelly couldn't believe it. As a kid she'd messed around with nitrous oxide, but only to make her voice go funny. Everybody did it, but she couldn't remember anyone passing out, never mind dying for fuck's sake. Mind you, none of her childhood friends were out of their skull on booze and crack at the time, like Jonny probably was.

"It'll be all over the papers tomorrow," said Jason. "I dread to think how they'll spin it."

"Fuck the papers," said Kelly.

Jason shot her a look, raised his eyebrows and vaguely nodded. She knew he wasn't judging her. It was more one of those almost-shrugs that signal resignation rather than disagreement.

"I was in the ambulance holding his fucking hand when he went," said Jason. He looked like he might collapse.

Kelly strode the few feet they'd been keeping between them and pulled him into her arms.

"You need to rest," she whispered. "Why don't you stay?"

Once Jason was in bed, Kelly slid in behind him. She reached round to his chest and pulled him to her. She hoped she was comforting him in some small way. It wasn't long until she could tell by his deeper breathing that he'd fallen asleep.

Kelly had no idea how much time had passed when she was woken by the sound of Jason sobbing. They must both have rolled over, because Jason was now behind her pressing himself against her back. He clutched her around her waist. She could feel moisture from his tears on her shoulder blade. She turned to face him. She kissed his wet face and murmured the kind of meaningless words and noises that people use to comfort grieving friends. Her consoling him seemed to release louder sobs. After a minute or two he quieted. Kelly found herself kissing his lips in the same gentle way she'd been kissing his face. Soon Jason was kissing her back, but not in his usual, urgent style. Kelly was aware that he was slower, more attentive. They were still under the duvet. As Jason moved on top of Kelly, he would normally have savagely kicked the covers off, or yanked them away. But he left the duvet in place, as if he wanted the comfort it supplied. He continued kissing her tenderly. She moaned when he entered her.

The minutes following were nothing like Kelly had experienced before. The climb toward orgasm was similar, but it was infused with affection and consideration on both their parts. It was such an all-encompassing and reassuring sensation that she found it incredibly arousing. She climaxed in a shorter time than she could ever remember. Jason came at the same time. Their coordination made the feeling of intimacy even more amazing. Before Jason moved away to lie on his stomach, he kissed Kelly once more, a light lingering kiss, so meaningful it made her tearful. As he lay, he kept one arm across her body, pulling her to him. Any chat felt unnecessary to Kelly. She lay quietly, feeling incredibly secure in Jason's warm embrace.

Kelly could see the almost full moon out of the windows facing the City. Didn't the moon rise in the east, like the sun? So, it couldn't be that late.

She thought about how difficult it was going to be for Jason. He didn't have too many close friends apart from Jonny. Kelly had been pleased when their plans for a documentary-making business seemed to be taking a more serious turn. She hoped he didn't go into a decline now that his prospective partner was dead. Although she doubted it — the enthusiasm for the business had been more Jason's than Jonny's. Plus, he had job experience and the MBA to go with it — with a bit of luck, and her urging, she was fairly sure he'd sort it. That is, if he'd still want to be around her when he woke up.

As she lay, listening to Jason's breathing, soft but steady, signalling to Kelly he'd fallen asleep again, her thoughts turned to her father. If she and Jason did get back together, she hoped to hell Frank could still talk him round. If Donovan was serious about the timetable for her 'recovery' and album production, she didn't have much time. Maybe she should just have another stab at writing some lyrics. Given her feelings for Jason at that moment, she could probably have taken a run at a love song. But that stuff had never really struck a chord with her. She'd found it easier to sing about difficult shit, like the pain of living. Maybe she should try to write a song about what a dick Donovan had been to her. Kelly smiled humourlessly at the idea but was aware of rising panic. What the fuck was she going to do?

When Frank phoned Donovan the next morning to suggest they meet for lunch, he threw in the delusional phrase his son-in-law had used on their last lunch meeting, "You know, just like old times."

"That'd be great, Frank. Yeah. Got to move a few things around, free me up for an hour or so, but no worries. Yeah, look forward to it."

Frank could almost hear the puppy-dog panting of anticipation.

Then, just before he put the phone down, Donovan said, "Great photos of Kelly, by the way. You've still got the magic touch with a camera, Frank."

Frank might have felt guilty — Donovan was too easy a prey, clearly chomping at the bit to get into his father-in-law's good books — but as it was, he couldn't wait to confront the little shit about Jim Healey. Frank was so pumped that even the snotty young maître d' at the Warwick didn't irritate him. He arrived early and demanded a round table in a corner of the room. He asked for two of the four chairs to be taken away. When Donovan arrived, Frank stood and indicated that his son-in-law should take the inside chair so that he sat with the wall on one side and Frank on the other. Once Donovan was seated, Frank moved his chair closer, leaving little or no room for Donovan to escape. Now he had Donovan where he wanted him, he could take his time. First off, he'd see what he could do to help Kelly. He'd been doing a bit of homework — amazing what he'd been able to find on the internet about record sales.

"So, tell me again what diamond means?" asked Frank, once they'd ordered their lunch. "How many of Kelly's album did you say sold?"

"More than ten million, give or take."

Donovan looked suitably smug.

"Christ, no wonder she can afford to live in that place," said Frank. Then he thought maybe he'd said the wrong thing, mentioning the penthouse. It might clue Donovan in as to why Frank was sniffing around about Kelly's earnings. Maybe he'd guess that Kelly had told Frank about the so-called loan. But Donovan seemed keener to downplay her income.

"You'd think so wouldn't you, Frank. But you have to factor in manufacturing costs, distribution, advertising, blah, blah. You wouldn't believe how small net profits are at the end of the day. It's a tough game, I tell you. Easy to get burned if you're not clever."

"Yes, but say an album sells for eight quid, even after all the costs, and after the retailer and the taxman take their cut, not to mention Canary Records slice of the pie, Kelly would still make at least a pound an album, right? And then there's all the other stuff. Royalties per play, there must be thousands, if not millions, involved there, right? And then the profits from the tour."

Frank was glad to see Donovan perform a few of his nervous nose-pulling tics.

"Tours only make money for the promoter, Frank," said Donovan, "The one and only reason for touring is to push the album."

He spoke so conclusively it was obvious he was trying to bring the subject to a close. He looked around as if to see if their food was on its way.

"Even it that were true," said Frank, which brought on more nose-pulling from Donovan. "There must be massive royalties. Every time you switch on a radio, you can bet that within fifteen minutes you'll hear a Kelly Anton track."

"Yeah, but that kind of frequency only lasts as long as

the album's in the charts," said Donovan dismissively, as though it was of no importance to anyone. Then he followed up, before Frank could speak. "Listen, Frank, did I tell you how happy I am with the shots you did. Fucking ace, they are. Never seen better of Kelly. Like I think I told you, you haven't lost the golden touch."

At that moment the waiter arrived with a basket of bread.

"Let's put the tour aside for a moment," said Frank, totally ignoring Donovan's arse-licking. "With record sales and royalties, she's got to have earned way more than ten million from the album, right?"

Donovan reached for some of the bread the waiter had left. He took his time spreading butter. It was clear he was regrouping.

"Look Frank," he said. "I don't feel comfortable discussing Kelly's financial situation. It's personal and private information. Sorry, mate."

He took a bite of his bread. But after a few chews, he couldn't resist taking a pull on his nose. Frank decided he'd rattled the little bastard enough about Kelly. He threw up his hands, knowing Donovan would read the gesture as him dropping the subject.

"Fair enough," he said.

But then, not able to resist one last dig, Frank added, "Just puzzled by a few things Kelly told me after the shoot, that's all."

"Kelly's a lovely girl, and a talented singer," said Donovan. "But she don't know fuck-all about business. And what she doesn't factor in is how much of her dosh has gone up her and Jason's nose ... or worse."

If Frank hadn't known better, he'd have been completely sold on Donovan's portrayal of Kelly as a full-time dope head. Maybe the more devious the person, the more convincing they were.

"I can't believe how quickly she cleaned up her act. She

seemed stone cold sober at the shoot. Clean as a whistle."

"Yeah, well, I take credit for that," said Donovan. "I really leaned on her. Tough love is what some of these temperamental artists need."

"Miraculous," said Frank.

Their food arrived. After a few bites of his 'rack of lamb with celeriac remoulade' — chops joined together, as far as Frank was concerned, and what was wrong with good old mashed spud? — Frank couldn't resist bringing up Whitney.

"She's doing alright," said Donovan. "I told her you'd done a fantastic job with Kelly's snaps."

"What did she have to say to that?" said Frank, trying his best to sound casual.

"Not a lot, but don't take it personal. What with the raging hormones and all, she don't care about much these days."

"What are you on about? Hormones?" asked Frank, unable to disguise his concern.

"You must remember, Frank, from when Christine was pregnant with Whitney, what a minefield it is. Mind you, she's calmed down a bit now she's in the home stretch."

Frank barely heard anything after the word 'pregnant'.

"You telling me Whitney's expecting?"

"Christ, Frank. I thought Christine would have told you."

"You know she won't talk to me. Why didn't you tell me when we met on the frigging bus the other day?"

"Honest to God, Frank, I thought you knew."

"When's she due?"

"A week or so," said Donovan.

The astounding news banished all thoughts of what Frank had learned from Jim Healey about Donovan and the ABH charge. He could barely eat. He was royally pissed off at his ex-wife for not being in touch about the baby, yet at the same time he was ridiculously delighted at the thought of his grandchild-to-be. Trouble was, he was also appalled to think of Donovan as the father.

"This is cause for celebration," said Donovan. "I fancy some sticky toffee pudding and a glass of fizz."

As they waited for their pudding Frank remembered the reason that he'd lured Donovan to lunch. Could he really stick it to his son-in-law, now there was a grandchild in the mix?

"Cheers, Granddad," said Donovan, lifting his glass of champagne. Something about his Cheshire cat smile rankled Frank.

"Cheers," he said. "Listen, Donovan. I met an old pal of yours last night. We had a long chat. You remember Jim Healey, right?"

When Donovan actually choked on his champagne, it occurred to Frank he couldn't have wished for a better reaction. Once he'd thumped Donovan a bit too hard on the back a few times, Frank laid it all out. He related how Jim Healey had told him about Donovan paying him to get Frank angry enough to lash out. That Jim had also said Donovan paid the man and woman to film the ensuing punch-up and to call the police.

"And what's more, Jim says he's always felt guilty about it, and since you never came through with the recording contract you promised, he's willing to spill the beans."

"He'll never do it. He'd be banged up for contempt," said Donovan. His nervousness had gone beyond nose-pulling. His face was white, freckles standing out like spots of dog piss on fresh snow.

"Jim says he doesn't care. But even if we don't get the law involved, I'm sure your bosses at Canary will be interested. Just like they'll be fascinated to hear about your misrepresentation of one of their top artists as a druggie."

Donovan pushed his dessert plate away, the pudding untouched. He glanced around as if looking for an escape route. It was obvious he'd twigged that Kelly had filled Frank in on their ruse.

"You think they'll believe her?"

"They may not, but when she produces Jason's hospital records that back up her claim you nobbled him and tried it on her too, so she'd look like she was off her head …"

"Jason's a frigging crackhead," interrupted Donovan, more than a note of desperation in his voice.

"Not so much, it seems," said Frank. "I did a little digging into our Jason. Did you know his father's a QC and his uncle's a high-court judge? They'd know all about defamation law, don't you think?"

He took the last bite of his dessert as Donovan stared at him, clearly panicking but lost for words.

"That was the best sticky toffee pudding I ever had," said Frank, once he'd finished. "You should try and eat some."

At that, Donovan broke. It was as though a damn had collapsed. He babbled on about never having meant to harm anyone. Surely Frank understood that it was just 'business.' When Frank said nothing, refusing to give an inch, Donovan became tearful.

"You was just so cold," he blubbered. "All I ever wanted was for you to give me the fucking time of day. Was that too much to ask?"

Out of the corner of his eye Frank noticed the prissy maître'd hovering, obviously worried that Donovan's meltdown might be upsetting the other customers.

Frank didn't give a shit about that, but he told Donovan as gently as he could to pull himself together.

"I was as upset as anyone when that to-do with Jim Healey got out of hand and you was given the suspended sentence," Donovan said, wiping his snotty nose with his hand. "After that, when you was on your uppers, I begged Whitney to let us help, but she wouldn't budge."

"Don't try to put this on Whitney," said Frank. "And

you weren't exactly helping me when you conned me into doing the photos of Kelly at the Catacomb, were you?"

"I know, I know," said Donovan. "It was my cack-handed attempt to get you on side, cosy up to you a bit."

Frank stared at Donovan. He'd seen unhinged people in his day, but they were usually having ego trip tantrums. This was different. Frank was no expert, but it seemed to him Donovan was on track for the loony bin if things didn't change.

"Listen, Donovan, if you really want to make it up to me, there's a few things you've got to do, all right?"

When Frank eventually stood, he pushed his chair under the table, as though considerately making space so Donovan could get out.

"Well, I think that was a very constructive meeting, don't you?" he said. "See you later."

Frank almost added the word "son," but given the obvious gaping wound he'd obviously inflicted at the wedding when he'd refused to acknowledge Donovan as such, he thought better of it. He knocked back his last swig of expensive bottled water and strode to the door. Frank waved a hearty, but he hoped an ironic, goodbye to the maître d', leaving Donovan to pay the bill.

He phoned Kelly as soon as he was back at FoodFoto. He didn't feel the need to give her all the details, but he told her the gist of what had happened.

"Donovan said he'd promise to drop the whole thing about you being a druggie. He said he'd do everything he can to make sure it'll all be forgotten. And when I said you'd want an independent accountant to go over all the figures on your last album he promised he'd drop the debt he was making out you owed … the cost of the penthouse and that. I suspect he's been diddling you left and right. So, the pressure's off. No reason you can't start in on a new album, right?"

There was silence. The phone line hummed almost inaudibly.

"You there?" said Frank.

"Did you talk to my Dad?"

"What?" said Frank.

"Did you square things with my Dad?"

"You do understand what I just told you about Donovan, right?" said Frank.

"Just tell my Dad what we agreed, that I'm clean and Jason is no crackhead," she said, and rang off.

Frank couldn't believe it. He slammed the phone down.

"Steady on, Sahib. Those things cost money," said Ali.

"I'm beginning to think Kelly Anton is an ungrateful bitch diva, after all.".

"Any more talk like that, Frank, and I'll set Rashid on you," said Ali.

Kelly turned from the phone to see Jason emerge from the bedroom where he'd been dozing all morning. She was glad to see he looked better — roses back in his cheeks, and clear-eyed — just like the Jason she knew and loved.

"Alright?" she asked.

"Yeah," said Jason.

Kelly was aware that she avoided looking directly at him. It felt almost like they were relative strangers the morning after a first-night fuck, not knowing what to say to each other.

They both started to speak at the same time.

"Look, Kelly ..."

"Jase, I'm so ..."

They both stopped and laughed, awkwardly, it seemed to

Kelly. But she was determined to have her say before Jason.

"Just let me tell you something."

But Jason didn't seem to hear.

"I should have been more understanding about Donovan and the enormous pressure he piled on you to produce a second album ..."

"No, Jason. You don't know the half of it. Please, sit down and let me get something off my chest, for Christ's sake"

"Okay," he said, and slid into one of his leather and steel chairs. Kelly sank in to the other one. She was having trouble breathing and had to suck in a great gulp of air before she could speak.

"The thing is, Jase ... I didn't write none of the songs on the first album."

"Whaat?" His forehead was deeply furrowed. He was obviously completely baffled. "What are you talking about?"

"My Dad wrote them, every word. I just wrote the music, but he gave me all the lyrics."

Jason stared at her in a way that made Kelly feel as if he couldn't quite remember who she was. A wave of panic swept over her at the thought that she was losing him again.

"It was something we'd always done, since I was a kid. Either he'd write some words and I'd come up with music to match, or I'd write a melody and he'd invent some lyrics to go with it. I'd performed them songs over and over in clubs and that. You saw me do them the night we met. I never thought to mention my Dad wrote them when I signed the recording contract."

"Didn't he mind he wasn't given any credit?" asked Jason. "I'd have been royally pissed off."

"He didn't seem to care. Just happy his little girl was a superstar."

Jason let out an exhalation of astonishment.

"But when those first reports of you and me being high appeared, and after he met you, my Dad was all upset, believing I was on something and I was living with a crack head. He wasn't inclined to write more lyrics for me. Then, when I stupidly made matters worse by going along with Donovan's ruse, he refused point blank, and we really fell out. So, I had nothing for the second album. Still don't."

The sensation, having finally spit it all out, was overwhelming. Kelly had often thought how wrong it was when relief was described as pouring into a person. To her it felt more like a great wave surged out of her. It left her feeling as if her backbone had completely lost its ability to support her. She slid deeper into the chair. But as Jason continued to stare at her, she began to tense up again.

"Well, say something for fuck's sake."

"It's incredible. He's brilliant. Those songs are pure genius."

The thought crossed Kelly's mind that Jason had never described the lyrics in such glowing terms when he was under the impression that she'd written them.

"I know. He's amazing," she muttered.

Jason stared at her. Affectionately, she thought.

"And this whole situation is mostly my fault, anyway," he said. "You didn't know what crack even was 'til you met me."

Kelly considered Jason's words for a few seconds.

"I mean you can barely handle a barley wine without getting giddy," he said.

"Fuck off," she said, but smiled.

She could barely believe it. She'd fully expected that he'd give her another lecture, at best. Walk out again, at worst.

They sat silent for a few minutes.

"We've got to fix this," said Jason.

Kelly told him how Donovan was putting it about that she'd gone through some kind of rehab and was suddenly all clean and was coming out with a new album.

"Frank's trying to sweet talk my Dad ..."

"Frank?"

Kelly explained how her father's old friend had turned up out of the blue, and how she'd asked him to help.

"... and my Mum will have told him by now that we've broken up."

"Have we?" asked Jason.

"You tell me."

"Course not," said Jason, grinning.

Kelly felt another wave of relief.

"But maybe you shouldn't let on. I could disappear for a while, let you and your Dad make up," offered Jason.

"Sod that," said Kelly. "I'm fed up with pretending."

Kelly hadn't felt so buoyant for months. God, but it felt good to have confessed all to Jason, and for him to have reacted the way he did.

"The only way through this is to come clean about everything to my Dad. You and me together."

"Fine by me," said Jason.

"I'll call Frank, ask him to set it up."

"Bring it on."

The next evening Jason phoned to say he was very sorry, he was running late, but that she wasn't to think he didn't want to see her Dad, just that the traffic was a bloody nightmare.

"No worries, but don't take the Albert Bridge or you'll never get here," said Kelly.

After she'd buzzed her Dad in, she began to wonder if the lift was broken. But then the doors finally opened and proved that the grey image she'd seen on the CCTV camera hadn't lied. Even in living colour, her father and Frank, standing side by side, looked like they matched. They were as tall as each other, and she was willing to

199

bet they weighed in around the same. They both wore black jeans and dark tops and each one bore the same pugnacious expression. Their serious expressions were putting her on edge.

"You look like bleeding twins," she said. She could hear the nervousness in her voice.

She was gobsmacked when her father burst into gales of laughter and Frank smiled broadly. Were they taking the piss about her obvious jitters, she wondered?

"That what wi used tell people when we out drinkin' after wi first meet," said her father.

Kelly didn't get it.

"One day, when we were working on the building site — where we met — we discovered it was both of our birthdays." said Frank. "In the pub that night, I started telling everyone we were twins. You should have seen the looks we got."

Nelson burst out laughing all over again.

Kelly smiled. Her nervousness eased.

"Same year too?" she asked.

"Yeah," said Frank. "We were both turning twenty."

"Forty-three year — gone in a wink 'o an eye,"

He laughed again and slapped his thigh.

"Come on in, then,' she said. "If you're coming."

They strolled out of the lift and slid into Jason's leather chairs.

"Can I get you anything?" asked Kelly. "Coffee, tea?"

"Line o' coke? Some E?" said her father.

"For Christ's sake," said Kelly.

"Take no notice, Kelly," said Frank. "I would have thought you'd know by now when he's joking."

"Not exactly a joking matter, is it?" said Kelly. "And it's not like we're in this pickle every day."

"I'm sorry dahlin'" said her father. "Come sit. I promise I'll be good."

Kelly perched cross-legged on the floor, which was perhaps a mistake. She felt like a little girl next to the two older men.

"Your Dad told me everything," said Frank.

"Everything?" asked Kelly, hoping to hell he meant what she thought he meant.

"Why didn't you tell me your Dad wrote all your lyrics?"

"I don't know," she groaned. She collapsed on her back in exasperation — with herself. She stared up at the penthouse ceiling far above her. "I was fucking stupid."

"Watch yuh mouth," said Nelson.

"I think because at first it was some kind of pride thing, like when you never want the other kids to see your Dad walking you to school," said Kelly, heaving herself back into a cross-legged position. "I was singing them for a while before the album, not thinking about him having written them, just trying to do the words justice. By the time I was recording I was so used to them lyrics that it didn't even occur to me to mention who'd written them. And then, I only discovered Donovan had credited me as the songwriter on the album cover after it was printed. It wasn't his fault. How was he to know any different.

"When the album took off, I did feel guilty, honest. But I was worried, if I said anything, it would cause a great big fuss, so I kept quiet," she said. "I did compose all the music, you know. — the arrangements. My Dad only wrote the words."

"Only?" said Nelson. "Listen how she talk."

"I didn't mean 'only' like it was nothing," said Kelly.

"I doan care about no credit. Nobody seein' no album cover anyway these days. But to mek out the lyrics be nothing." Nelson made a loud tutting noise with his tongue against his teeth that Frank remembered was his way of showing everything from disapproval to annoyance.

"Obviously, without them — without you — there isn't any Kelly Anton, multiplatinum, diamond, whatever, recording star. I've tried writing lyrics, but they're always shite."

"It isn't just me," said Nelson, ignoring what Kelly had said. "She never want show Ruth her contract, neither. Free legal advice, sitting there for the takin', and she get screw if we even suggest such a thing."

"He means annoyed. I'd get annoyed, thinking they thought I didn't know what I was doing."

"I hate to say it, Kelly, but you didn't," said Frank. "Know what you were doing, I mean. I bet Ruth would have picked up on all kinds of stuff Donovan had in there to diddle you out of thousands."

"I know that now, don't I?" she said. "But when you're a nobody and someone offers you a recording contract, you feel overwhelmingly grateful. You definitely don't want to rock the boat making demands. And anyway, you trust the bastards will treat you fairly … or the bastard, singular, in this case."

"I presume the singular bastard — a.k.a. Donovan — still doesn't know it was Nelson wrote all your songs?"

"No," said Kelly. "The longer it went, the harder it was to tell him. Even when not telling him landed me right in the shit."

"And I never want claim it were me. First, nobody believe me, and anyway, me no want mi own daughter to look stupid."

"I tell you Nelson, that one you wrote about being outside or whatever was bloody brilliant," said Frank. "How d'you know about those feelings anyway?"

"We no talk 'bout mi lost years yet," said Nelson.

Kelly felt a pang of resentment, but now wasn't the time to confront her father about his fuck ups before she was born.

"Exactly, he's a bloody genius. That's why, without him,

I've been totally freaked about coming up with a new album."

"Look, love. It true I been a bit harsh, but I took that bwoy for a drug-addict loser. And you can't blame me, after seeing all the newspaper stuff, for b'lieving you was goin' down the same road. The only way I thought might change you was if I refuse to work wi' you. But you so pig-headed …"

"Well she was in a bit of a bind by then," interrupted Frank. "With Donovan making her believe she owed him money, she had to go along with his insane scheme."

"And I did try and explain that Jason's no more of a drug addict than your pothead pals, no matter what the papers might claim."

"Where he is, anyhow?" asked Nelson.

At that moment Frank heard the sound of the penthouse lift door opening. A slight but tall, young man with a shock of chestnut red hair appeared.

"'ello, love," said Kelly.

"This here is Frank, an old friend of my Dad's. Frank, Jason."

"Pleased to meet you," said Jason, in a voice that reminded Frank of Prince Harry's.

Despite the awkward situation, there was an air of easy confidence about Jason that Frank had seen before in young men from a certain class. Frank didn't believe the class system was dead by any means. It might be that money was the new yardstick, and there were all kinds who'd become super-rich. But the majority of the rich were still more often than not from the old upper classes, with their attendant, inherited wealth — and their sense of entitlement.

Even if Frank was off the mark about Jason's pedigree, one thing was certain, he didn't look like a druggie. Jason was fair-skinned, especially in contrast to Kelly, but he didn't appear pallid or unhealthy. His skin had an unblemished quality, which suggested clean living as well as fine, Celtic blood. His hair was tousled, but not unkempt. It was in the same purposeful disorder as Kelly's, which must have taken some effort to achieve, presumably involving gel or whatever people used. He was watchful, regarding Frank with a cool gaze from clear, azure eyes, but not in the sly, deceitful way of an addict looking for his next fix, like blokes Frank had encountered in the hostel he'd lived in when he was down and out.

"And you know my Dad," said Kelly

Nelson stood and, Frank was relieved to see, he not only shook Jason's hand but rested his other hand on Jason's shoulder in a friendly gesture, before sitting back down.

Jason settled himself on the white chaise longue.

"Is it okay if I call you Nelson?" he asked.

"It a bit soon yuh call me Dad, so yeah, is okay," said Nelson.

Jason looked slightly bemused.

Nelson erupted in gales of laughter.

Jason grinned.

All Frank could think about was his rubbish reaction when Donovan had asked if he could call him Dad, at his daughter's wedding. It wasn't the first time he wished to hell he could go back in time and do things differently.

"How did you and Frank meet," Jason asked, once Nelson stopped laughing.

"That a long story," said Nelson.

"Go on, tell him," said Kelly. "It's wild what happened."

Frank decided, if the story of his youthful fuck-up was going to be told, that he'd do the telling. When he'd finished, Jason let out a low whistle.

"Amazing. I can't imagine how terrifying it must have been for you, Nelson."

Nelson said nothing but appeared glad to have the horror of being wrongfully accused of murder acknowledged. He closed his eyes and nodded. There was silence for a few seconds, but any awkwardness had dissolved with Frank's telling of their story.

"Are you from Birmingham originally?" Jason asked Frank,

He'd obviously spotted the last trace of Frank's Midlands accent.'

"Good ear," said Frank. "Wolverhampton, actually. You?"

"Birmingham. I lived there when I was a kid, before I went to Repton."

So, Frank had been right. Years at a public school like Repton would supply a posh accent, if the family hadn't already drilled one into little Jason. Although the school had some oddball old boys. Frank seemed to remember Jeremy Clarkson whining on about being bullied there. Probably accounted for his own bully-boy tactics.

"My parents live mainly in Edgbaston," said Jason.

Frank wasn't familiar with Edgbaston, but he seemed to remember it was one of the well-heeled areas of Birmingham.

"Mainly?" he asked Jason.

"They spend most of their time in Scotland. We have a place in the Highlands."

Frank thought the use of the word 'we' was a clue to a family with a lineage of some sort, even if it was only a couple of generations. The use of 'we' was quite a contrast to Kelly's referring to the house in Jamaica as her "Dad's house," even though she'd paid for it. Frank was willing to bet Jason's family's Scottish 'place' — whatever the word meant — had been in the family for a while. It was

205

likely it would one day be Jason's, unless there was an older brother in the mix.

"This all well an' good, but you and me better get to work," said Nelson to Kelly. "Frank told me we don't have much time."

"Yeah, we've only got a month to come up with enough for an album," said Kelly.

"Come then, we go back to the house," said Nelson. "Wi need the piano when I tell yuh all these songs I got ideas on."

"Now?" said Kelly.

"What more you got to do but make music?"

They said their goodbyes to Jason. This time Nelson gave him a full-on hug.

"Yuh smell good, bwoy," he said. "Clean like sea breeze."

On the way down in the lift Nelson said to Kelly and Frank, "It weren't that bwoy's fault his family was in the slave business. And Ruth'll come around sooner or later 'bout them being posh so."

When Frank winked at Kelly, she smiled so brilliantly that he almost wished he had his camera.

SIX WEEKS LATER, Frank, Nelson, Ruth and Kelly trooped into the front door of Canary Records' office in Soho Square. Kelly had begged Donovan for a two-week extension of the month deadline he'd given her, so that she — and, unbeknownst to Donovan, Nelson — could finish writing, and she could compose music for, the dozen songs they'd come up with for the new album. Kelly was due to start recording the following day, so Donovan had called her in to sign her new contract. Despite being less bitter about his son-in-law's actions since their lunch together,

Frank couldn't wait to see the look on Donovan's face when they all showed up and told him exactly how things were going to proceed in the future. He just hoped Donovan didn't have a break-down on the spot.

Frank was also feeling less hostile to Donovan since his reconciliation with Whitney. He'd been totally and pleasantly surprised when she called him to ask if he wanted to come to the house and meet his new grandson.

"Donovan told me you'd stopped drinking. He said it was time we buried the hatchet," she'd said.

Frank was quite emotional when he saw his little girl nursing a newborn baby. She shushed him when he launched into a tearful apology for past behaviour. He managed to keep shtum when she tried to explain Donovan's bad behaviour away by telling Frank he had a massive hang-up about not having a father.

"He thought you'd be the answer," she said. "When you wasn't, he went a bit doolally."

Frank must have looked quizzical.

"Okay, that stunt he pulled what put you in court was psychotic. But I never knew about it "til he confessed it to me just recently, you know that, right?"

Frank had felt slightly put out when he found himself reassuring Whitney that she'd done nothing wrong, when he'd thought it would be the other way around. But he let it go. Maybe all those hours of anger management had had some effect after all.

"But he's having counselling," Whitney had said. "And now he's a father himself he's promised never to do anything so stupid again."

The upshot was that they'd played happy families ever since. Frank wasn't wild about the name Ziggy, but if that's what they wanted to call his grandson the last thing he'd do was make waves.

So, given the recent warm and fuzzy family feelings,

207

Frank was feeling slightly concerned about sticking it to his son-in-law. But Frank was ninety-nine percent certain Donovan wouldn't risk screwing up his and Whitney's being back on good terms by whining to her about their business negotiations. And everything had to be agreed by Donovan and Canary Records for Kelly's sake, before she cut the new album.

Once inside Canary's building they were told by a long-haired young man that Donovan was on a phone call and wouldn't be long. They were shown into what was described as 'the boardroom.' The place was done out like a Las Vegas interior designer's idea of what a traditional British boardroom might look like. Thick burgundy carpet, man-made fibres glistening in daylight streaming through floor-to-ceiling windows that overlooked Soho Square. Dark-stained oak veneer everywhere, from wall panels to lumbering furniture. An unnecessary array of gleaming brass studs outlined blood-coloured fake leather on huge chairs ranged around a cricket-pitch-sized table. If Frank were cynical, he might believe the room was designed specifically to intimidate impressionable young musicians into signing away the rights to their work. But Frank was more amused than threatened. And Nelson and Ruth certainly didn't appear uncomfortable, they pulled out a chair each and sat, appearing relaxed as if they were sitting around their kitchen table at home. If anyone seemed freaked, it was Kelly. She hovered at the window, head swivelling, clearly looking out on, but not seeing the square below. When the door opened, she started and turned quickly.

"Bloody 'ell, Kelly. I never knew you 'ad a gang," said Donovan, looking around at them all in surprise, teeth bared in a nervous facsimile of a smile. "Bit old for gang members though, in't they." Frank was gratified to see a couple of frantic nose pulls. Donovan was clearly perturbed, despite his show of bravado.

Frank noticed a visible change in Kelly. The fluttery manner she'd had while they were waiting was replaced by a resolute stillness. She had the same bearing and expression she'd had on the stage of the Catacomb before she sang. She'd stared out at the crowd, appearing to grow in stature, as if challenging them not to be impressed. He realized her earlier jitters must have been nervousness before the performance she was about to give. She stood for several seconds, staring at Donovan as if sizing up a combatant. Eventually she shook her head dismissively.

"Frank here is now my manager. I believe you two talked … at a recent lunch at the Warwick pub? Where you discussed a certain saxophonist, Jim Healey. And I believe the subject of Jason's father and uncle came up too."

Her tone of voice was more business-like than menacing, but it was perfectly clear to Frank, from Donovan's expression, that he knew he'd be in danger of losing her if he chose to challenge her, or anything else she had to say.

"Nelson Clarke here is my songwriter," Kelly continued. "He's written all the lyrics for the new album … as he did for the first."

An expression of astonishment bordering on panic crossed Donovan's face. He seemed so taken aback he forgot to pull on his nose.

"And this is my lawyer, Ruth Barton. She has a number of alterations to accounting practice and also some corrections and additional clauses we want incorporated into the piece-of-shit contract you sent for me to review before coming here to sign."

Even the Soho traffic outside seemed hushed. The silence stretched on for seconds, during which Donovan stared from one to the next.

"One of the clauses has to do with performance rights," said Kelly. "It specifies no more arena gigs or big boffo tours. I only want to do smaller venues from now on."

Donovan looked like he might throw up.

"But without the tours, how the fuck are you going to promote the album?"

"Our technical wizard, Ali Khawaja ... "

At the name, Frank noticed that Donovan's forehead furrowed. He was obviously trying to remember where he'd heard the name before.

"... has come up with an idea for doing one-off internet concerts," continued Kelly. "With enough advance notice, we'll have gazillions watching, not just the few thousand you'd get in an arena. With links to downloads you'll make millions of instant sales."

Donovan couldn't have appeared more stunned if Kelly had slapped him.

"Kelly, there's just one more point," said Ruth. "I think Donovan needs to know I'm petitioning for retroactive royalties for Nelson from the first album."

At that, Donovan shrunk into his massive chair, where, being so diminutive, Frank thought he resembled a wayward child beaten into submission.

"Oh yes. Thanks for reminding me, Ruth," said Kelly.

"So how come Kelly signed with that tosser Donovan again, even if she did get all she wanted? Him and Canary Records stand to coin it with this new album, innit," said Ali.

Frank couldn't help feeling slightly awkward. For one thing, he still felt vaguely out of place in the amazing live/work loft where they were sitting. He'd only taken possession a few weeks earlier. Before that, he'd hardly heard of Dalston, let alone imagined himself living there. But he'd been told the area was 'the new Chelsea,' whatever the hell that meant. And, as well as having an airy and separate living area, the place also provided more than enough space for his photo agency, as well as for an office for Jason.

He supposed he should call it his and Kelly's agency, even if she was only a silent partner. She'd insisted on bankrolling it when he'd let slip it was what he was aiming for by working at FoodFoto.

"Christ, Frank, you'll be dead and forgotten before you can save enough," Kelly had said when he initially refused her generosity. What clinched it was when she added, "Anyway, you and Ali will be working for me some of the time, and we'll need somewhere Jason can get his business up and running."

Frank, who'd always been used to working solo, thought he might have trouble being part of what Kelly called "her team." He worried he wouldn't be able to hide any irritation he might feel. But so far there'd been absolutely nothing to get on his wick. Kelly gave him pretty much free rein on any management decisions. Donovan had proved to be immensely helpful, once he'd realized Frank and Ali's fresh ideas would mean increased album sales. Ali was so happy to be out of their dark cellar at FoodFoto that he forgot to be sarcastic. And he was proving a genius at marketing Kelly in unconventional ways. Rashid put it down to Ali's total ignorance of how things had been done in the past.

"He's like one of them 'idiot savants' innit," said Rashid.

Try as he might, Frank couldn't see any reason things should ever go wrong.

"Truth be told, it was me persuaded Kelly to stay with Canary," Frank told Ali. "After all, they did sell a shitload of the first album. Just that they didn't pay her her due, but that's all sorted for the second one."

"And in business you can't let them personal feelings cloud your commercial judgement," said Rashid.

Frank had been delighted when Rashid agreed to join them after he and Ali had told Bertie Big Bollocks where to stick his jobs and left on the spot. With Ali handling the tech side, the scanning of images and storage, and Rashid helping with sales — at least until he finalized a deal on his digital goggles with one of the tech companies who were vying for the rights — Frank was confident his photo agency would be up and running in no time.

"Actually, there was a bit of the personal thing going on too, to be honest," said Frank. "Donovan is the father of my grandson, after all."

"Nothing wrong with mixing business and family," said Rashid. "Just as long as they's capable."

Ali frowned slightly and looked sceptically at Rashid.

"Wot?" demanded Rashid. "Just 'cos your family is in-capable." He put the emphasis on the 'in.'

Frank was puzzled, what the hell were they talking about? He must have shown it, because Rashid explained.

"Ali's moved in with me, but his family is none too pleased."

Frank thought he knew what Rashid was implying, but he was glad when, astonishingly, Ali made it clear.

"By 'move in' he means living together ... as a couple."

"A gay couple," said Rashid.

Ali squirmed slightly. Frank was glad he could take the news in his stride, having suspected for a while they were more than just friends.

"I'm sure your folks will come around in the end, parents usually do," said Frank. "But enough of this chit chat, we should get to work. Or my partner, Kelly — Ali's new girlfriend — will have our guts for garters."

Frank winked at Rashid.

"I should be done calibrating that scanner in an hour

or so," said Ali, seemingly oblivious to Frank's teasing. Probably because Kelly did seem genuinely besotted with the IT genius after Ali had come up with the digital concert idea and other plans that he'd dreamed up for her.

Another string in Frank's recently acquired bow of projects was helping Jason with his documentary company. When Kelly, Frank and Jason came to check out the place before signing a lease, Frank had been chatting casually to Jason about his plans for the business.

"Would you have time to work with me on it?" Jason had asked. "With your experience you'd be incredibly helpful."

"I don't know a lot about making moving images," Frank had said.

"It can't be that different, I know of at least two still photography shooters who ended up making commercials, even features," said Jason. "And you know about rights and royalties."

Frank had conceded it wouldn't be a huge jump, and he'd been having second thoughts about selling the entire collection of his old stock ever since his revelation on the bus, when he'd recalled the MailOnline photo editor's disappointment that Jason hadn't died. He realized he couldn't live with himself if he sold any of his pictures that showed people at a time when the last thing they wanted was to be photographed. Frank hoped that working with Jason could supply income he'd lose if he culled his photos down to just responsible content.

After he, Rashid, and Ali had transported all Frank's files — transparencies, photoprints, and negatives — to the new space, Frank had gone through them all ditching ones that might show anybody in a bad light.

"But when we went to shoot Kelly, you claimed it was them sort of pictures what made the most money?" Ali had said.

"I know, but we'll make plenty off the rest. We don't

need to sell shite like that."

When Ali looked doubtful, Frank had said, "Think of us in terms of the organic food you're so big on, we'll only sell stuff that won't do anybody any harm. And with our share of Kelly's album sales for managent fees we'll do alright. Plus, when Jason's production company takes off, we'll be in clover."

Ali had been sceptical about Jason to start with.

"I hope he won't be doing crack in the lavatory," Ali had said.

"Jason's clean, apparently," said Frank. "Kelly said he hasn't touched anything but the occasional beer since that friend of his died."

And now, after almost a month in the new space, Frank found it amusing that Jason and Ali were comparing their tastes in music like new best friends, despite their obvious differences.

"You sorted what pictures you want me to scan first, yeah?" Ali asked Frank.

"Believe me, Ali, I've been planning that every night for a very long time."

"What we waiting for then?" said Ali. "Let's do this!"

THE PAPARAZZO AND THE POP STAR
Copyright © Andrew Smith 2022
ISBN: 9798364314215
AXIOM PUBLISHING

The moral right of Andrew Smith to be identified as the author of this work has been asserted in accordance with the Copyright, Designs and Patents Act of 1988.

All rights reserved. No part of this publication may be reproduced, stored in a retrieval system, or transmitted in any form or by any means, electronic, mechanical, photocopying, recording, or otherwise, without the prior permission of the copyright owner. All characters in this book are fictitious, and any resemblance to actual persons living or dead is purely coincidental.

www.andrewsmithwrites.com

Manufactured by Amazon.ca
Bolton, ON